New York Hates Your Face

R.B. Winters

DEDICATION

This life has been made possible by a
lot of wine and really good friends.

New York Hates Your Face

Table of Contents

New York Hates Your Face

Preface

Could the world continue to turn without the existence of this book? Of course. *New York Hates Your Face* is never going to be viewed as a great literary work or a must-read in any classroom. Actually, the use of profanity is probably enough to have the book banned in a handful of states. Which may lead you to the question, why inflict this collection of essays onto the world?

This book is meant to share a handful of experiences which I wish I had been informed of before moving to New York City. If you are anything like I was at twenty these lessons will all fall on deaf ears and will mean nothing until you look back in a few years. More or less making the entire book a fruitless effort on which I should give up now.

To the point: Unlike the pretty picture painted in television shows and innumerable blog posts, New York is sort of an asshole. This city will kick you every time you're down, spit on you and then laugh as you try to pick yourself up and move forward. That's the point, this is not a place for the weak. Maybe the city isn't as rough as it was back in the 1970's, but the rising number of hipsters and boutique coffee shops has not diminished this place and its ability to take the wind from your lungs and drain your mind of the will to live.

My hope is that by the end of this book you'll have a realistic glimpse of what it's like to live in the city. If you already live in New York, I hope you're laughing along and nodding your head, comparing the stories and commentary to your own experiences. That being said, this book has a bunch of inappropriate language, short stories and ridiculous and totally not, politically correct information. All of this is obviously from my point of view, which is the way I prefer.

Read and enjoy, and at the end, you may just realize how great New York City is and love it with the same fervor as I.

1. #NYHYF

Taylor Swift, Global Ambassador for New York City, sings, *'Welcome to New York, it's been waiting for you,'* when in fact it has not. A better title and chorus for this song would be something along the lines of: New York hates your face and nobody cares that you're here.

Now, you're sitting here with a gaping mouth thinking, *how can this cynical asshole speak foul of Miss. Swift* and, even worse, pass judgement on her city. In truth, I love me some T-Swift as much as the next overexposed, pop culture consumer. I have the albums, sing the songs and even attend the occasional concert.

Actually, funny story, a friend and I attempted to attend the Taylor Swift concert in Toronto this past fall. It was something of a meeting point between our two home cities. I bought the concert tickets and my friend reserved the hotel room. No concert would be worth the time and effort without drinks. We located a bar offering a happy hour special a few hours before the concert, conveniently close to the hotel, and began to drink.

The wine had different plans for our evening, leaving said friend face down in the hotel toilet while I found entertainment downstairs at another bar. We both missed the concert because she was passed out and I refused to go alone. In my mind, I'm way too old to be alone at a Taylor concert, everyone would probably think me a pedophile as well as a sad creepy old guy. Probably worth noting, I enjoy the random story in the middle of a thought, so get comfortable, there are many more to come.

Back to popular culture: Cram the corporate music down my throat and tell me it's good, I believe you. But my point remains valid, New York City is not interested in anyone who arrives on her doorstep. If you've ever met a native New Yorker they may very well inform you, no length of time can make you a true New Yorker, fortunately pop culture to the rescue, be it, Sex and the City, declared ten years the magical number. Thus, we transplants yearn for the day when we reach the big 1-0 and can forever shed our former selves and proclaim victoriously, "I am a New Yorker, mother fuckers!" This is not to say it will be easy. Nothing worth having is ever easy, right? I think that's the saying people use to torment others into not giving up, so let's pretend we're optimistic and buy into the concept.

So, Taylor's song, which I do enjoy by the way; You see, this song was created, in my mind, for consumption by someone who has no idea what the real New York is like. Living in a $20 million Tribeca loft is not the real New York. When Taylor has lived in Brooklyn, not Williamsburg, the real Brooklyn, way out in the middle nowhere, a.k.a. near the end of a train line, get back to me. Coming to New York in your twenties means arriving with no money, no job, some sort of education if you're lucky, and then shacking up with one to five roommates in an apartment that's too small and too expensive. That's New York, and I wouldn't have it any other way. Skipping these steps leaves you unable to appreciate the struggle of building a life here. Sorry, Taylor.

I myself was once the starry eyed twenty-something who moved to the big city with just shy of two-hundred dollars in my pocket, a car full of crap and no place to live. Technically, I spent my first few months renting a room in Jersey City with a sweaty, bald guy who loved to stand in the doorway and talk my ear off while eating bowls of oatmeal. He was perfectly harmless, but annoying nonetheless. This gentleman made me work hard to convince a friend to move to Brooklyn. It had become painfully obvious I couldn't live with a total stranger, they don't understand when you tell them to not speak that it's not rude, it's necessary for survival and mental sanity. Oh, well.

I'm Brian, probably should have mentioned this earlier. I also use the names, Ryan, Richard, Bobbie and occasionally Alex. Names to me are just like an outfit, you can put one on and be whomever you wish. This is one of those things you learn coming to the big city, suddenly it's possible to be whomever you want. No longer are you tied to the person you were born and raised as, unless you choose it to be so. There is still some part of the twenty-something in me who can look back as a new thirty-something and say, I survived. *Thank, Jesus!*

So, what is the point of all this rambling and Taylor heretic talk. My goal is to share what has proven to be a hilarious, disastrous and sometimes painful point of view on what it really means to be a New Yorker. No, I will not be telling you of beautiful weekends spent in the Hamptons and rent controlled apartments. Maybe if this book has a sequel and by then I've been adopted by a wealthy, old Jew heiress on the Upper East Side, I can share those stories. I'm not there yet, unfortunately. What you're going to get here are the Coney Island trips, falling in cellar shafts and bruised egos that come with the city. By the end I think you'll love the city just as much as I do. Unless you're a completely rational person, then your reaction may be more along the lines of, *'Why, God, why?'*

Where better to start than at the beginning, well, right after the beginning because I already mentioned the time spent in Jersey City. I'll only add Journal Square [Jersey City] is one place anyone can get robbed, stabbed or shot. Unless it's changed, who knows, they clean up neighborhoods once in a great while. So, the start, which can only be one place: Brooklyn.

Once upon a time a twenty-year-old kid from a small town called Hoytsville (it's a real place, look it up) dreamt of life in the big city. In his mind, there was but one city, and that was New York City. Popular culture pumped him full of ideas and sensational possibilities of an incredible life which could be lived, through shows like FRIENDS and Sex and the City. The characters enjoyed such wildly exciting lives and proved it was possible to love a city like a person. The idea was thrilling, even intoxicating, to someone who had literally been nowhere in the world.

I hear you scoffing about the show selection, but be honest with yourself, you've watched both. You probably even watched the finales with friends and shed a tear or two. Let's leave the judging to me, at least for now, and get back to the story.

So, this small town boy packed up his car with all he could fit and set out on an adventure. **INSERT JERSEY CITY CLIP HERE.** Once he realized a proper roommate, not a creepy Craigslist person, would allow him to move into New York City proper, our small town boy convinced a friend from back home to make the move as well. Brian and Lacee searched for apartments until they found one Jewish landlord who was willing to rent to two, terrifyingly white twenty-year-olds.

Oh, the apartment was perfect, a two-bedroom railroad layout in a newly refurbished building. What made this apartment even better was the location, East Williamsburg. It was only a hop and a skip from Manhattan; where we all truly prefer living and existing. A lie you will often hear from people is how much happier they are living in Brooklyn and Queens. Not to say people are unable to enjoy these quaint boroughs, but no one has ever moved thousands of miles, only to end up living outside of Manhattan permanently. You notice this more as people move into Manhattan and begin to reveal how they truly felt about their former boroughs.

At this point, I'm going to go ahead and switch out of the third person, it's starting to sound weird in my ear. After moving all of our stuff into the apartment, we made a call to turn on the power; ConEd informed us the building wasn't listed. This is one of those perplexing moments when you don't know how to respond. The customer service person claims the building doesn't exist, but I'm standing in the building of which we speak, and there is literally a gas meter in the basement with a signed meter reading tag from ConEd. This parlayed into needing paperwork from the building manager for reasons which are still not clear. This was the least complicated issue we would face, of course, we had no idea at the time.

Summer, specifically July, in New York City is the hottest, most humid time of year, when suicide or a pool are the only two acceptable options for tolerating the horrific heat. Our new landlord was less than helpful in getting the power turned on. My roommate of the time, Lacee, and I sat in the dark on our first night in this new place, sweating and eating melted ice cream and Spaghettio's from a can. Truly the finest in white trash dining experiences. The best we could do was put cold washcloths on our heads and try not to pass out from the oppressive heat.

The days were long as we fought with the landlord to get what the power company needed to map the building and provide the luxury of electricity. We lived like squatters for nearly a week and getting an electric current wasn't the only issue. The toilet in our shiny, shiny bathroom had so much old, dried shit from the construction workers crammed inside, that when we turned the water on it didn't clear the pipe. Trying to unclog the toilet, first with a classic plunger, we flung literal shit, all over the walls and ourselves. A disgusting experience that still causes me to dry heave. You can't forget some smells. Going so far as to buy a drain snake we finally had to give in and call a real plumber. We did call the landlord for help, but seeing as they didn't care about the power, they certainly didn't give a shit about the actual shit.

Life without a toilet is no party, Lacee at one point had to have her period in the bathtub. Coincidentally, this is the first and only time I've ever seen what comes out of the opposite sex. Did they teach this in Sex Ed? Unfortunately, when my school taught the class I was out sick, and they don't really care if you make up the class. Maybe that's why I've spent so much time asking all of these sex related questions…but that's a different story and another book.

Desperate times call for desperate measures. Aside from the period issue we were showering at the gym and in Starbucks bathrooms like the homeless, all while running around town looking for outlets to plug in our phones. Every outlet was always full in every bar, restaurant and coffee shop. Could it be that every twenty-something in New York was going through the same thing? Were we all living in new apartments without power and water? Or, perhaps everyone was without air conditioners and spent their time in these cool retreats. We may never know the truth.

Shit aside, we learned really quick what East Williamsburg actually meant. The neighborhood name is how real estate agents at the time tricked white kids into moving to Bushwick. Present day Bushwick is partially gentrified, and where we once lived is now becoming trendy. When Lacee and I called Bushwick home, we were the only white people in the surrounding area.

Now, if you're conservative, politically correct, or any other obnoxious thing I refuse to tolerate, this is the trigger warning for the rest of the book. I'm going to be saying things like black and white. There will also be some god damn, fuck, cunt and I'm sure a bunch of other remarks you'll dislike. Feel free to put the book down, light it ablaze and walk away…if you can. Would it be completely tacky to insert a smiley face emoji here? Yes, it probably would, but know that I want to.

Back to the point: Our neighborhood had some scary black people. To make you feel better about the term black I will give you this: As a white, gay guy in a bad part of Brooklyn, it was fairly common for the black guys congregating on street corners to scream *'faggot'* at me as I walked to/from the train. See, we all discriminate against one another. Being one-hundred and thirty pounds at the time, I kept my mouth shut and eyes down. The last thing I needed was to get my face bashed in and end up in the hospital. Except once on Halloween when I was dressed as a rape victim and slightly intoxicated. I may have started yelling back and it was only because Lacee shut me up and shuttled me along that I didn't get my ass kicked.

Lacee had her own unusual encounters with the neighborhood locals, like when she got off the train one night and a man sat on the ground outside the station stairs sharpening a machete. Apparently, this is a perfectly normal activity to perform on a city sidewalk. Oh, and the constant pandering from guys interested in her ass. If you are a white girl and you have a butt you will certainly attract attention, more so from black men because they love ass for some reason. Even as a gay, I'm not that interested in ass, I especially can't understand why straight men love lady ass. I mean, Amy Schumer said it right, *'that's where my pooh comes out.'* Kinda gross if you think about what you're obsessed with, though I didn't exactly make a great case for being gay here either. We can just pretend this paragraph never happened.

It wasn't only the black people who didn't like the two white kids infringing on their territory. One Dominican man robbed our apartment three times before we realized what was taking place. Technically, it was twice and the third time was cut short.

Robbery one: Lacee's laptop and other items went missing. Having only been in the apartment a few days, still living out of boxes and without power it was possible she just hadn't unpacked everything yet, and the issue was temporarily disregarded.

Robbery two: Two weeks after the first missing laptop, I was out for a job interview, returning home exactly four hours later to discover my laptop missing. I knew exactly where it was sitting when I left the apartment, and upon my return it was nowhere to be found. The worst part was the evening before I had finished writing a book after more than two years of work. Is that cosmic punishment for something or just a bit of bad luck? After having a near breakdown, and reporting the theft to the police, things went back to normal.

Robbery Three (Sort of): Two weeks later, always two fucking weeks, I was home in bed around noon, having been out all night drinking. I wasn't working at the time, no need to be up early on a weekday.

A banging started, so I rolled over and tucked my face into the blanket, doing my best to ignore the disturbance. When it didn't stop after a few minutes I got out of bed, mind you, my bed was a blow-up mattress and a single blanket. Walking to the front door, the banging came again before I could reach for the knob, clearly coming from Lacee's room. Pushing open her bedroom door, to my surprise, a man had his leg and head inside the window, which was twisted on an angle inside the frame.

Stunned, we glared at one another for a moment before the thief bolted up the fire escape. Standing there in my underwear, it took a moment before it occurred to me to call the police. Obviously, they were too late, and actually caused excessive damage when ripping the window the rest of the way out of the frame. At least our criminal was polite enough to gently remove and replace the window, leaving no sign of entry, with each of his visits. It pays to be good at what you do.

The police told me there wasn't a chance in hell I'd see the laptop again, which didn't stop me from going to every nearby pawnshop for the next couple of weeks, hoping it would be there just waiting to be rescued. The cops which responded also left us with a little piece of advice that scared the hell out of me. They said to be careful in the dark hallways of the building, as it was common for crackheads to jump out and stab you. What, are we on an episode of Law & Order? I mean, the halls were painted in thick black and red stripes, like something from a Freddie Krueger movie, but they weren't scary until this bit of knowledge was shared. It did force us to pay a lot more attention to the hallways, up until the point which power was provided and lights installed.

This is what you can count on when moving to New York, if you experience the real side of the city and not just the rich part which certain people enjoy when they come as outsiders and claim to be New Yorkers. It's going to bark and bite, you just have to be willing to take it and start barking back.

2. Apartments

There are a few common ways to leave an apartment. The way generally forced upon society is to put in your notice, find a new place and vacate the premises with only a small amount of damage left behind, such as nail holes and scuffed floorboards. New York offers many more ways to leave or *lose* an apartment.

There is the eviction, a way in which I prefer to avoid in life, but it happens to people all the time. You can't afford the rent this month? No problem; get the hell out. Your credit will be ruined for years and you'll end up paying the rent in the end, as ruthless bill collectors hunt you down and make endless phone calls to intimidate and torment, but eviction is one way the landlord or management company can cut their immediate losses.

To be fair, eviction isn't always cut and dry, apparently if you have a child or are knocked up, it's not possible for the landlord to kick you out, even if you are behind on the rent. I only know this because Lacee shared the details after we stopped sharing an apartment and her landlord asked if she was pregnant or planning to be in the near future.

Inappropriate landlord questions aside, there is a much more terrible way to leave an apartment. For example: Suddenly your roommate is getting a rash, it seems like no big deal, we're all allergic to everything these days because the Internet has told us so, what's a little red flesh when you think about it? Well, when the roommate's rash isn't going away and you too flare up with one, it begins to seem like more than a mere coincidence.

If you are like Lacee, you may do some summer closet cleaning and spread your belongs out on the bed in an effort to organize. If you're like me, you'll put on the old black Halloween wings that have been hiding in the closet, toss a red thing over your head, then run through the apartment yelling, *"I'll get yo' baby."*

To put this in context, the lady who moved in across the hall had a newborn. The baby was a demon sent straight from the depths of hell to punish me. We shared a wall and a love of the evening, me and my bed, the baby and shrill screams. It cried, cried and cried all night...every night. I fucking hated that thing, but never played the card of rude neighbor who complains. I get it, those things are hard to control and shaking it only lands you in jail.

One sunny day, I was home in the afternoon playing the stereo, I can't recall what was playing, but I can say with certainty it was something poppy from the late 90's. A knock on the door only to reveal the neighbor from across the hall asking me to keep it down because she'd just put the baby down for a nap. Again, I understand your child and I are forced to coexist in this world, but I refuse to have my life altered because you failed to use a condom.

I ever so politely informed this person, I would not be turning the music down, seeing as I never complain about her baby keeping me up at night. To boot, if she kept the baby up in the day it would actually sleep during the night. Our spat ended with me slamming the door in her face, though the night crying did cease after this point. It's amazing what can be accomplished when you tell someone to fuck off.

Fuck is one word you will become well acquainted with as New York takes hold of you. Fuck those tourists blocking the sidewalk. Fuck the MTA for trains never being on time and making you late, even though you left your apartment ten minutes after you should have already been somewhere. Fuck that weirdo looking at you across the bar. You get the point, yay for fuck!

Anyway, after our fit of laughter and the wicked wings came off, Lacee pushed some of the hanging clothes to one side of the closet, only to reveal a massive patch of blackness. Turns out there was a leak behind the wall, which was not properly fixed during the building's renovation. The leak made its way through the sheetrock and formed lovely black mold, and we were now breathing it in on the daily.

When we called the Jewish landlords, they told us to call one Jew, then another, then another, then another. I'm not sure

I've ever used fuck on the phone in a conversation as often as with these men. It boiled down to abandoning the apartment and taking the first available place we could find, while fighting to get the deposit back from our look-the-other-way mold-lord. I strongly feel we had a legitimate reason for now wanting to stay in the apartment and expecting our deposit to be returned. Also, language in the lease clearly stated the tenants have the right to leave if the apartment isn't livable. It's funny how our Jewish friends are all about contracts and the included lingo until it doesn't work in their favor.

If you've ever had to find an apartment in New York City, then you understand it's like a game of Russian roulette. If there's something you like, it's important to sign the lease papers and put down a deposit immediately. If you leave the apartment to think about things, there is a 100% chance someone will view the apartment later the same day and take your new digs. Since our money was tied up in the mold apartment, there wasn't much we could work with financially, deposits are usually about three month's rent, so we ended up in Clinton Hill. A cute part of Brooklyn with lots of local charm, but the apartment was literally slanted, a little too much charm for my taste. The first time I spilled water on the kitchen table it ended up across the room. Another example of our building's tilt, when you filled up the bathtub, one end was full and the other half empty. This was disappointing, mainly because I'm always down for bath time.

The apartment had several other interesting features we didn't truly notice until fully settled. One feature, the previous tenant was some kind of mechanic/hoarder who never moved out of the place. Having abandoned the apartment, the landlord didn't bother moving this guy's stuff out and assumed we'd just happily do it as part of our move in process. This translated into throwing piles of sharp metal crap, tools, busted up furniture and more into and around the trash bins in front of the building. This in turn pissed off the super who tried yelling at us in Spanish, only to discover it wasn't our shit before giving us a break. He turned out to be a really nice man, and is still the favorite among all the supers I've had. Once he even helped me dig out the stairs to my apartment, the one after the place mentioned above, when a super snow storm buried my door under four feet of white hell.

After we cleared the junk and started scrubbing away the layers of dirt, it became evident the bathroom was lacking a sink and a mirror. I have no idea how we missed these features originally, perhaps it was the stress of the situation or lack of experience in finding places to live. The only sink was that of the kitchen, a large silver industrial type of sink covered in smears of paint from the previous tenant(s). At least one of the former tenants was a painter of some sort. Even if the painter wasn't the last guy/gal, who left us the giant mess of metal to move, his or her presence was felt.

Harnessing the spirit of our dirty paint sink we painted the kitchen bright orange, my room a neon green and Lacee's room a sky blue. Our apartment looked something like a clown's pillow after a night of intense drinking, which ended by crying tears of remorse from jerking it to non-clown porn. I feel most clowns are probably sad, mainly because they spend their days scaring the hell out of people like myself. Also, they have to tolerate children at all times. Saintly in act, horrible in reality.

Things did mellow for a bit after our big move extravaganza. That was until another rash appeared on my ribs. This one was different than the last and itched nearly as bad as the chickenpox, which I'm an authority on, having had them on three different occasions. Anyone who tells you chickenpox are a one and done disease are liars and should be shot in the face.

This new rash was so irritating, I went directly to the doctor, convinced he was going to tell me the issue was something related to AIDS, or some other horrible thing I may have contracted by working my way around the block. Anytime I catch something funny I think I have AIDS, no idea why. The doctor was unable to identify what my issue was, but did note the rash was caused by bites, most likely from a spider or something similar.

The rash came and went and it was only because one night, while in bed with the flavor of the week, when my back began to itch that everything became clear. Getting up, walking to the bathroom where we had recently installed a small mirror, twisting around to see what was so itchy on my shoulder blade, I saw a weird little bug. With a firm slap the bug exploded, blood smearing my fingers.

Rushing back to the bedroom, flicking on the light as I tore back the blankets; There in the sheets were other little dark bugs. It was the worst of all possible things: Bed Bugs. Now, if you've never had bed bugs, you can't understand how truly horrible they are. Think of it like this, you'll be more willing to tell strangers you have herpes than bed bugs. People back away from you in an effort to not be contaminated with your blood sucking vermin. Never again will it be cute to hear: *Good night, don't let the bed bugs bite.* Though my mom thought this was a funny joke while we had the things.

Getting rid of bed bugs is almost as confounding as figuring out where they came from in the first place. Lacee may have brought them to us from her Harlem boyfriend's apartment, confirming that's where she first saw them. They could have also come from the Chinatown bus I took between Baltimore and New York on the regular, but we'll discuss that in more detail later…maybe.

Once we confessed to the landlord our pest problem, he sent over a lengthy checklist. There are a dozen things you must do before an exterminator will even step foot into your bug infested apartment. It's recommended you discard any cloth and paper materials you can. This includes bedding, clothing, furniture, books, really anything inside an apartment. There is a misconception that bed bugs only live in the creases of mattresses. Nope! They live pretty much everywhere. In the walls, between wooden floor slats, bedding, closets, dresser drawers, they will make any and every space of yours, theirs.

We tossed everything we could out, including the air mattress I was sleeping on at the time. What remained had to be placed in massive black trash bags, sealed and sent out for cleaning. When the exterminator finally graced us with his presence he shared that there would need to be several treatments spread out over a few months, and he couldn't guarantee the results. Did you know the main chemical once used to effectively kill bed bugs is now illegal because it also kills birds? It's true, and because of this we get to suffer through the use of inferior, though toxic, chemicals which don't always solve the problem. Let the damn birds die! Especially if those birds are pigeons. Those winged, rat bastards are more annoying than the morons who feed them.

Suffice it to say, the apartment drama and bed bugs stacked on top of a long commute and work stress eventually soured the relationship between Lacee and I. She moved out and to the Bronx, I moved out and to the apartment in the basement of the same building. It was a bigger, cheaper, darker apartment with all kinds of bugs I've still never identified, but it was home...for the moment.

Eviction may be the most threatening of ways to leave an apartment, but having to abandon one due to bed bugs has to be the most painful. The way you should leave an apartment, to ensure your sanity and credit rating remain intact, is by providing aforementioned notice and then beginning your apartment hunt two weeks before your lease ends. You'll likely have one to two weeks where you have two apartments, but it sure as hell beats spending a night or two on the streets...especially if you have to move in the winter.

One last thing that cannot be overstated, when it comes to picking an apartment: Amenities. This is of course going to be dictated by your income. To be clear, almost all landlords, management companies, and general overlords controlling our lives, require you to make an annual income that is forty times the rent. To quickly do the math, think of it like this; In order to have an apartment which costs $2,000 per month, you must have an income of $80,000 per year. Feel poor yet?

The amenities of a building are nearly as important as the location. Some people go for the doorman buildings. Personally, I find this to be a huge issue. Yes, it's nice to have someone who can accept your packages, because God knows UPS is incapable of delivering a box during the time which they say. Case and point, when I ordered my espresso machine from Bed, Bath & Beyond, the UPS guy left it in front of the building door, on the sidewalk. The box had the store logo in giant letters, so of course someone stole all the contents from the box. The best part, this was delivered a day early, which would usually be a benefit, except if you're not planning for the box to be early, then there is no way to be home. Do not pick a doorman building simply because you need someone to collect your junk, get a post office box. A doorman will know all your dirty, late night [dick sucking] secrets. Just saying, it's something to think about.

The amenities which are worth holding out for include: In-building laundry, rooftop deck/outdoor space and elevators. Having recently moved from an elevator building to a six floor walkup, I can tell you from experience that an elevator is vital to survival. Do you know how heavy even the smallest box becomes when you have to carry the thing up ninety-two steps? You'll have an ass for days, but you'll also want to throw yourself from the window to avoid walking down the stairs and up again. Yes, to amenities, yes to elevators!

3. Dating

Some people come to New York with the expectation of finding love. The likelihood of finding love goes up if you're willing to settle, but goes way, way down if you're looking for something specific. The city is full of people, some are nice, some are dicks and others are pure evil, placed on this Earth for the singular purpose of causing you a horrific dating experience which will be burned into the back of your memory for years to come. *Warning: Date at your own risk.*

So, what can you expect as far as dating? Well, there are the nice guys (and girls, but I don't know much about them). These are the guys you'd want to take home to your parents. Sweet isn't the right word to describe these gentlemen. Not only are they available to you, by which I mean they'll travel from their borough to yours without questions and reply to every text within minutes, but they're also more or less addicted to you. It doesn't take long before you begin to feel smothered and the butterflies in your stomach begin to die, replaced by a gut wrenching fear of what's to come. These are the guys who want to commit. If you can last more than a few weeks with one of these dudes it's likely you'll end up sharing an apartment, getting married and saddled with children. At which point you'll grow your drinking habit into a problem and begin sleeping with Bob from the office. Why Bob? Because it's always Bob. It's also important to note that someone who will leave their borough for you is pretty damn romantic. It's right up there with someone who is willing to give you their seat on the subway.

After a few nice guys, you'll become aware of what to watch out for and find yourself interested in the exact opposite. If there's an asshole within ten meters, you'll be able to spot him and find yourself incredibly attracted. It won't matter if fifty of the most gorgeous, nice guys are blocking the bad boy, your senses can cut right through them. You want the bad apple because it's sour and tastes good.

You may share a drink with Mr. Bad, or even a meal: Once. Following the first "date" you'll spend countless nights sending text messages only to receive one word replies, often coming hours or days after the original message. You'll find your new relationship turning into more of a fuck buddy situation, seeing as you'll only see this guy at three in the morning when whatever plan he had suddenly falls apart, or he finds himself turned on without an outlet for release.

The asshole guys are worth avoiding to a degree, but they help you thicken your skin and learn to tolerate so much more than just bad dates. These guys teach you how to disconnect from your feelings and treat sex as nothing more than a casual encounter. Every therapist ever will say this is a horrible statement. They're probably right, but they're also the ones usually in bad marriages who sleep with patients and still send you a bill. A free asshole is better than an overpriced hooker any day.

There is however, one rare and elusive individual who you may come across once, or twice, if you're lucky; The datable guy. Not an asshole and also not a crazy person who attaches to you while confusing love with sex depravation. You'll meet and have a great first date. Usually it goes so well you find yourself questioning if you're crazy, reading things wrong and perhaps it was an awful evening. Then he'll reply to your text messages, he'll make plans for a second and third date, he may even meet some of your friends. You'll be in a state of bliss with a side of confusion. This guy is defying all dating logic.

At this point it can go one of two ways. Either it works out and you've found something real, or, as is usually the case for myself and those around me, the guy meets the real you and runs as quickly as he can.

An example which recently happened to me (If we can't exploit our own humiliation, what good is it doing us?):

Having met a guy through one of the many mobile dating apps on my phone, we met for a quick drink. The conversation was engaging and the night rather enjoyable. He reached out for a second date, this turned into several dates, and even a day trip to Brooklyn one Saturday afternoon. I love Brooklyn, even when it's a dick to me, everyone should visit.

The skeptic in me was a bit confused by this guy, he didn't seem to be following the dating rules of New York City. That was until about five weeks in when one of my lady friends and I went out for a happy hour. Rebecca and I were celebrating a long week coming to an end with half-price wine at Bistro 61, a little French place on the Upper East Side. I planned to meet good-date-guy later in the evening, nine to be specific. Around eight I pinged him via text and informed him I was feeling pretty good. I was drunk in case you're not comfortable with the use of subtle language.

Apparently, the number of times I was allowed to be myself had just run out. He informed me he didn't wish to continue seeing me. This all started off friendly and even my drunk self was being polite, though stunned. That was until he started to explain his efforts were aimed at trying to make me feel good about myself because I'm, "pretty." This was confusing and incredibly aggravating. You don't tell someone you hope to never see them again and begin patronizing them.

Being drunk, I quickly moved from calm and rational to less than polite in my responses. Note: This is still all happening via text message. I miss the days when we could fight in person, or at the very least, scream at each other over the phone in the back of a cab. In no uncertain terms I told him go fuck himself. To which he let me know how sorry he felt for me, "…because I'm a self-hating, drunk."

He was really just stirring the pot at this point. I'm probably a drunk by most normal standards. If I open a bottle of wine, there's a pretty good chance I'm going to finish the whole thing. When a friend invites me out for happy hour, I say yes. When there's a party and someone wants to go, let's go. The whole point of being young in New York City is to enjoy. Correction, young or old, the point of being in New York City is to have fun, do crazy shit and have experiences. If I wanted to play it safe and live by the rules, I would have stayed in Utah and gotten on board with the Mormon family, baby making thing.

As far as being self-hating, I suppose that is how someone on the outside could perceive me. I'm bitter and cynical to no end. Though this is what makes me fun, or at least it's what makes me fun in my own head. I believe it is because I'm not interested in accepting someone's compliments, and focus more on achievement for validating worth, that this guy arrived at his misguided conclusion. This however is merely speculation as I didn't ask why or how he came to have such opinions, frankly, I didn't give a fuck at the time. Minor correction, I still don't give a fuck, but it would have been worth finding out 'the why,' if for no other reason than to expand this story to a proper conclusion.

For me, Dan (I wasn't going to use his name, but who the hell cares.) will now go down in the history of my dating life as the datable guy who passed his expiration date. Though I do look forward to the inevitable point which we will run into one another. We know several of the same people and one of his friends is a regular at one of my friend's parties. Like any good, bitter person, I've racked up a dozen perfect first exchanges, but time will determine when, where and if they ever exit my mouth. *Oh god, let it be soon.*

You're reading this, hopefully with a bottle of wine [because I'm writing it with a bottle of wine], and thinking, *why would anyone date based off of these terrible observations?* We have to. That, or reserve ourselves to lives of vigorous masturbation. No matter how many bad dates one goes on, one is always inclined to go on more. It's not just our brain telling us to do so, it's also our phones. There are dozens, if not hundreds of dating and sex apps that can more or less ensure you avoid becoming a crazy cat person by connecting you with other weirdos. For the record, I only have one cat, my friend Rachel has beaten me to the crazy cat point by having seven...and she never uses the dating apps. I love her and all her pussies.

It's not all bad dates I admit; you can meet some people who turn into great friends from dating. In fact, I believe dating is the only reliable source of discovering rejects who you'd be interested in befriending. It's true, almost anyone you meet who has lived in the city for a few years will tell you, they first went on a date with one or more of their closest friends.

Those are the dates, where none of the guys described previously, are the one you're sitting across from at the bar. These are the quirky ones you have a ton in common with and get excited to see. Then on the second date, or third if you're conservative, [I'm not] you attempt to have sex and it's an epic failure. The kissing is off, they're touching you in weird ways and if you're a girl, you're glad you can fake an orgasm or your period because this has to end. Speaking of faking, I wonder how many guys out there fake an orgasm? I've only managed it once because the lights were off and I pretended to cover my business with a hand. After the bad sex, if you make it to the end, you won't talk to this person for a few days, weeks or months and then you'll come together, forget the past and start a friendship. It's like magic, it also makes little sense, but that is generally how it happens.

I digress; Dating in the city sucks, it's probably one of the worst things you're going to experience. But you'll keep doing it, in the vain hope of meeting someone special. You'll also do it because you're pissed at the one friend you have that's been with someone for a few years, and you are determined to prove you are not socially retarded and are actually capable of love. I'm speaking directly to Rebecca and Eric now, a.k.a. the Straights; How do you do it? Seriously, if you two weren't in a relationship I'd assume you'd been lifelong friends. That sounds all kinds of sentimental, so I'm going to stop now before I ruin the chapter. Though, I do plan to get completely bombed at your upcoming wedding and be highly inappropriate. Rebecca, tell your god-loving-mama, she's my primary target for inappropriate, alcohol fueled commentary. Oh, and shirtless, there will be no shirts worn as you are wedding at the beach. Nipples, vows and your mama!

4. Friends

You know the feeling when you move to a new place as a kid and suddenly, it's the first, terrifying day attending a new school? Everyone is a stranger and you're flying solo. It's one of those unpleasant things we all dread and hopefully only experience a few times. That's kind of what it feels like to move to New York. People here are actually rather nice when you get down to it, but no one is here to help you or make life easier. They're busy and have things to do, which doesn't include babysitting a newbie.

Making your first friend is incredibly difficult, for me, it was a date which brought along the first friend. As previously mentioned, dating is a great way to find friends, be sure to make a note. I will add, this may only be truly effective in the gay world. I've spoken to some lady friends and putting a guy in the friend zone sounds much more problematic when you are straight. Maybe the difficulty factor of making someone a friend is increased by their position on the scale of heterosexuality.

The Animator, as I call him, and I had a few dates and things never really went anywhere, but we had a good time and made each other laugh. I mean, anyone who is willing to watch horror movies and eat inappropriate snacks, registers high on the list of people I am willing to tolerate. All these years later, we're still friends, and it just so happens he was the unintentional catalyst for a majority of my other friendships.

I believe the most effective way to make friends is to collect them from other people. Obviously, you have to make a first friend, and we all manage to get over that hurdle at some point. Animator decided he preferred being a recluse over the past three years, becoming a bit of a flake and bailing on people left and right. On this one occasion, the beginning of the flake period, Animator invited me to go on a wine tour with his friends, out on the North Fork of Long Island. I didn't want to go because everyone was already connected and I'd be the only outsider, but I sucked it up and went anyway.

Not much of a surprise, in hindsight, Animator no-showed. He technically didn't cancel, pissing off his other friends and leaving me to navigate the waters alone. This is the point where you more or less start freaking out inside your head. What do you do with a bunch of strangers? This is a moment of dread for people like me. Being in a situation where you're totally out of the comfort zone and trapped for several hours makes you want to tell everyone you have diarrhea and need to get home.

What I learned from this experience is the most obvious thing, something which you probably already know if you're over the age of twenty-one. You can make friends with anyone if you drink enough. Three vineyards, several hours and too many bottles of wine later, it was the beginning of two new friendships, the Russian and Larrymore. This may have turned out very different if Animator had actually shown up for the wine tour. I likely would have stuck by his side, talked mainly to him and kept away from the others. Sometimes you have to get out of your comfort zone to make friends, I hate it as much as you do.

Animator is also responsible for my friendship with Business. If you can't tell by now, I enjoy giving people nicknames. Not only does it save me from lawsuits as I write, but it provides just enough cover so only the inner circle of people know who is who when it comes to books and blogs. Business and I had met a number of times through Animator at happy hour and other drinking events. I recall him introducing me to his friends, before we were actually friends, as 'the funny guy.' I take this as a huge compliment, funny is hard to pull off, and it's one of my favorite ways to be described.

Business is my best example of a collected friend, as we never went on a date or anything of the sort. We began grabbing beers after the Animator was no longer interested in playing. When I say 'playing' I mean going out for drinks and antics, which needs to be clarified as most people assume it means sucking dick or some other adult activity. Business is probably my most faithful friend when it comes to drinks. If I need someone to go out for a beer, he's the man. Though, I rarely drink beer these days as it leads directly to a beer gut. *Wine, please!*

Things are a bit out of order here as my friends Larrymore and the Russian first really connected with me on the wine tour. This was way after I became friends with Business.

The Russian and I did have one date, both of us fitting the other's type. It's a perfect example of two people who are awesome as friends, but would probably never speak again if the relationship had to be rooted in dating chemistry. We went for beers, and didn't have much to talk about, followed by a peck on the subway platform and several weeks of silence.

These two are the duo, I lovingly refer to as, 'my/the Gays.' It is through them I met my other important duo, 'my/the Straights' which were previously mentioned. My male and lady straight are a couple who not only can put my liver to the test when it comes to brunch, and other competitive drinking adventures, but they're also a damn good time. The names may not make a ton of sense now, but as we continue to weave in and out of stories the pieces will become clear.

All of this is convoluted chatter, but it's the best way I can illustrate how the friend connections happen in New York. For someone like me, who works from home, it's impossible to meet people through work. Who am I going to meet sitting on the couch, a hooker? Even then, it's a business transaction, not friendship. The only other people I engage with on a daily basis are the baristas at Starbucks. Even though they know my name, it's safe to assume they could care less about seeing me outside of our four-minute daily encounters.

Still, why tell you all of this? You need friends in New York. You need people who are native and those who moved here prior to you. The native New Yorkers will help you learn the proper lingo. For example, a common mistake of the Western person who has moved back East is to say, "We were in Long

Island." No, it's never 'in' it's always 'on' and a native will not be shy about correcting you. Same goes for lines: You stand on line; you don't stand in line.

Natives also help you really learn the city. What's where, what's cool, etc. They don't do this by getting out a map and pointing, it happens by making plans to go out with them. You'll learn really quick how vital it is to master the subway, and even more important, how to tell a cabbie where you live. Not so much a problem today, but a few years back, if you told the cab driver you were going to Brooklyn, they would toss you back onto the street without blinking an eye. Regulations have made them more compliant, or friendlier, if you want to call it such.

Transplants, like myself, are just as important to your New York experience as the natives. These are the friends who will reminisce with you about where you're from and reaffirm the decision to leave was the right one. For example, my lady straight, Rebecca, and I like to have white-trash-offs. We exchange our white trash stories to see who had the trashiest childhood. It's all very healthy.

For example, Rebecca (Don't sue me for using your real name, now that I've done it a half-dozen times.) grew up in New Hampshire, with a crazy religious mother. I grew up in Utah, with a crazy religious [cult like] society. Not so bad, thus far. Rebecca grew up in a double-wide mobile home, she beat me there because we only had a single-wide trailer. She was living large by our poor standards. With all our stories, I try my best to win or come in a close second, it's the competitive nature of a city dweller.

Let's see for me: There's the aunt and uncle who went to prison for a meth lab in their barn. The schizophrenic uncle who also suffered from gigantism later in life and died thinking "they" were coming to get him. Sister with two kids by eighteen, and the brother who is nearly forty and has spent more time living on sofas than working. Between my parents I've had two step mothers and two step fathers and a number of step siblings, I think it's seven or eight at this point.

This is the kind of stuff your native friends may not be as interested in hearing about, as it's drastically different from their life experiences. Transplants can sympathize and help you laugh about the scary roots you've shed.

One thing Rebecca had that I didn't, was a toilet in the front yard used as a planter for flowers. I've seen them, but she is the first person to admit to having one, or at least admitting her family had one. If I recall, her uncle also lived in a shack behind their trailer on the same property. Though we had this discussion in Puerto Rico over several drinks, so I could have mixed some of these facts together with things seen on the street that day.

Even more important, and this is one of those rare moments when I won't drown the commentary in cynicism, the friends you make in New York, the real friends, are the best people you're ever going to meet. They'll put you in a cab when you're shit face drunk after a night of dancing away a breakup. They'll hold onto your spare key, so when you storm out of an event in another state and ride Amtrak home in the middle of the night, you have a place to stay and a way to get into your apartment. They'll even help you move, or at least give you the number of a decent moving company.

These are the people you want to invest your time in above all else. Before and after the dates, your friends are the people you can plan on seeing ten plus years down the road. Just hope you have friends like mine who hate children and don't have plans to inflict them upon the group. Alright, just that one bitter comment. Children do tend to ruin friendships if one half of the group is anti-baby and the other is pro-baby.

Things won't always be perfect; you're going to have some fights. What makes fighting with other city dwellers difficult is the reality that there is no right or wrong way to fight. You can go fist to fist like the pub crawlers, and knock some teeth out before savoring a beer together. You can scream at each other and get the problems out in the open. As a reactionary person, this is usually my method of choice. You scream, shout and twenty minutes later move on with life.

There is one method of fighting, which I've recently received a dose of that is particularly difficult. Silence. What the fuck do you do when your friends decide to stop talking to you? Let me back up as you'll need some context here. Last February, I was vacationing with a few friends in San Juan, Puerto Rico. It was sunny, warm and the idea of moving to this beautiful island came up.

Returning to New York after the long weekend away, I proposed the idea to friends. All summer, I talked about moving to Puerto Rico for the winter and avoiding another freezing New

England season. Cold and me do not get along, maybe it's because my last name is Winters.

Fast forward to a week before my scheduled departure. I had a dinner with my straights friends and plans with my gays for brunch. Seeing as nothing ever goes according to plan in life, it turned into a hectic work week that didn't allow me adequate time to pack and prepare. Halloween, my favorite of all holidays, was the only opportunity I had to pack my shit up and get my apartment ready for the tenant who would be moving in the next day, as I left for six months of sunshine. My inability to say 'no' to work and not getting an early start on packing, meant cancelling brunch plans with my gays. I did cancel three days in advance, as I could see the timing issue coming as the work piled on early in the week. They were not pleased. I agree, they had the right to be mad that I cancelled. A reasonable amount of anger would last one to two weeks…in my opinion.

Fast forward three months and one of my gays was still ignoring me. I guess I can't say he's ignoring me as I have stopped putting in any effort to talk to him as well. The other gay does talk to me on occasion, but I get the impression he only does so when he is nowhere near our other friend and I'm sure it's a tightly held secret. The silence was temporarily broken a few weeks back when I blogged on the topic. What can I say, I love picking at an emotional scab just enough to make it bleed.

I more or less wrote the above in explicit detail, which you can find on my website noted at the end of this book. Yes, I'm plugging my own work within my work. The blog post received an anonymous comment from the friend who was freezing me out. His point being that I didn't inform him I was moving and didn't make a point to see him before leaving. Oh, and there was some business about me putting more effort into seeing the straight friends and not the gays friends.

I replied with what I believe to be the truth. Since I began talking about this move seven months before it actually happened, it seemed there was fair enough warning. Yes, my final week did not consist of an effort to see people. I didn't move. I live on the Upper East Side and still have my apartment ready and waiting. Wisely, I sublet to save a little money while I'm away on a beach. If I was eighty-years-old, this would make me a snow bird, but because I'm thirty it's moving and crazy for some reason.

Now that I had my friend in a battle of words and he had an opportunity to tell me his thoughts, it was only fair to fire back. I believe he has too many strings attached to his friendships. For example, he pushed the straights away because he claims they didn't invite them to his wedding. They told us to save the date a year in advance, and in fact, the invitations went out seven months after that conversation. I'm sure the gays will not be surprised; they've been officially uninvited for their cold shoulder to the straights.

Now, my one gay claims, he just expects his friends to include him in their decisions and it's not about strings. If you aren't dating me or paying my bills, then you get no say in any decision I make. Does anyone really feel differently? I mean, getting advice from friends is important, but only you can make the decisions that are best for you. It's like we walked into the Bad Blood video, which I fully approve of; Thank you, Miss. Swift.

You're probably shaking you head and thinking how ridiculous this behavior is. I fully agree. Not to say I'm blame free, but I can tell you this, all this time has passed and some of us are having a great time together, while others are still offering up the silent treatment. What is my point here? Actually, I should ask, what is the lesson here? No matter how well you know people, how much time you spend together, or how close you are, in this city the only person you have is yourself. Don't forget to make friends with yourself or you're fucked.

We will touch on this more later on in the book, as there is a vicious two-year cycle which can claim and destroy your friendships and this fits the pattern perfectly.

5. Transit

The subway. Oh, the subway. The first time you enter the New York City Subway, it's sort of like attending your first gang bang. No one makes eye contact with you, you're being shoved around, it's a million degrees in the summer, ice cold in the winter, you're feeling lost and confused. What's worse, the first few times you pop out of a station, you'll glare around at the streets, with no concept of where you are or where you need to go. The massive stone structures stretch upwards forever, people continue to filter by as if you don't exist, and you deliberately avoid asking for help; After all, you're not going to look like a tourist.

When you first arrive in New York, assuming you're not Taylor Swift, meaning you don't have millions and millions of dollars, you'll be forced to get familiar with public transportation. Now and then you will spot a celebrity on the train, *because they're just like us.* Except for the reality that their ride is usually a photo-op.

Once you master this complex network of stairs, tunnels and tracks, you can pretty much get yourself to any obscure part of New York City, as well as a few places you'll likely avoid ever visiting a second time.

This is not to say you won't get lost a few dozen times. When Lacee and I were rooming together in Brooklyn, the A train was our lifeline to and from the city. We also had the option of taking the L and the G trains, but more often than not, the A was the winner of our uninvited escapades.

One of our first attempts at taking the train home, after a day of romping around the city, went slightly off track. It does take some time to become familiar with individual subway stations, beginning to notice the subtle differences from one to another. Not all stations are drastically different in design, and none of them are the same in layout.

We should exclude some incredible abandoned stations from the above statement, such as City Hall, which you can see if you stay on the 6 train at the final stop, Brooklyn Bridge. The City Hall station is truly unique with its curved platform and vaulted ceilings. The 6 train loops through the defunct station to head back Uptown, offering you a rare glimpse into the lavish stations, which are now nothing more than history. There's also the 18th Street Station; If the 4, 5 or 6 trains are going slow in or out of Union Square, you can see the old platforms. Today, covered in graffiti and dirt, most people never even notice them through the tiny windows. There are many more abandoned stations and tons of videos of people [illegally] exploring them. Definitely worth a Google search.

Now, it should have been obvious to Lacee and I that we had missed our stop, once the number of people on the train began to thin. In actuality, what led to us believing we may have gone too far was not the lack of people, but the fact those still on the train were giving us dirty ass stares. Apparently, two preppy, white kids were not so very welcome in this place. It was at this point we exited the train as soon as the doors opened, clueless to where we stood, only knowing this was a station neither of us had ever seen.

Deep into Brooklyn, we had gone many, many stops too far. It was late in the evening and all we could do was laugh at ourselves for being stupid. Eventually we made it home, because the one thing you can depend upon with the MTA is that the night service is hit or miss, but it is always running. At the time when we stood on the platform there were no countdown clocks to indicate when a train would arrive next. Once in a blue moon you might hear a barely audible announcement of a train. If the train was actually coming, shrug.

This sounds like no big deal, so we missed our stop, but made it home in one piece. I agree, not such a big deal, the point is a majority of your travel pain will be self-inflicted and usually involving the A train. Like the time I was coming back from a trip and leaving JFK [airport], only to see the train pulling into the station. It was nearly midnight and rather than hope for another train, I bolted, luggage in hand, as fast as I could move. Passing through the train doors just as the ding rang out and they slid shut. Plopping onto a seat, catching my breath, I leaned back to relax as the ride home was a solid forty-plus minutes.

Parts of Brooklyn and Queens still have elevated rail and the subway isn't actually a subway, it's just a train roaming the cityscape. For this reason, my mistake was not immediately obvious. With headphones blasting it wasn't possible to hear any of the announcements from the conductor, not that I wanted to hear the garbled words. Then we pulled into a station where plywood was covering most of the platform. Assuming renovations had begun in the week I was away, it was paid little attention. Twenty minutes later the train stops, all doors open, and I'm the only one in the car. Finally, I took a moment to read the sign and learned I'd taken the A train to Far Rockaway. This is the last stop in Brooklyn on the train. Let it be known the only thought in my head was: ***Fuck me!***

These are some of the adventures you'll be able to look forward to as you learn the system. These days my time is consumed by the 4, 5 and 6 trains, being that I live on the Upper East Side; Brooklyn a memory, just a stone's throw across the river. The 6 line is one of the most congested in the city when it comes to straphangers. **Fun fact:** A straphanger is the proper name for a subway passenger, stemming from the days when leather straps hung from the ceiling and were used by passengers to steady themselves during the commute. *Learning is fun.*

One of these days we may have a Second Avenue Subway line, though this train is somewhat of a myth/legend that's been in progress for decades. If it does actually open to the public in December of 2016 as planned, this information will be irrelevant. So, my train is the 6, the one JLo named an album after, while conveniently leaving out the torture of a commute all riders experience. You know the train is crazy, when a random woman stabs a stranger for no known reason, while exiting at 59th Street. Yeah, that happened a few years back, look it up. You could probably search Google for Bloomingdale's train stabbing. Bloomingdale's happens to sit right above the 59th Street station, so you expect a little more tact from passengers. Like, if you're going to attack someone, pushing them in front of the train would be more acceptable than a non-fatal stab wound.

Applying effort, as in, getting to know your way around will make life cake. I mean, as far as travel. If you don't have a decent job and money, your life will probably be painful and suck to a certain degree, but that's the case in any major city. Once you have the hang of the subway, you need to learn the appropriate onboard behaviors. Are you looking me in the eyes? Why are you staring at me, you fucking psycho pervert?! This is the facial response you'll receive any time you stare at people on the train or bus.

Keep your eyes fixed steadily on the floor, out the window or at your cellular device. The one time you forget this rule, is going to be the time someone is having the worst day of their life. They're going to confront you and get in your shit. Seeing as you're likely from the Midwest or West Coast, you'll be shitting your pants, because no one prepared you for the confrontational nature of a New Yorker. Treat this like a bear attack and coil into yourself. Let them finish their rant and change cars if possible. Remember, you don't want a knife through the ribs.

Also, probably more so for the ladies, be aware of men who will try to grind their junk into your backside. As well as the guys who will try to give your ass a little grab. There's one in every bunch, you never really know who it will be, but they're there. As far as touching goes, you also have the people who slide their hand down the pole to rest upon your own. The only thing you can do is move your hand above their hand. If you slide down, so will they, again and again. Go ahead, play their sick game, you have no idea where their hands have been. I've seen enough men texting at a urinal to know, most people are carrying some funky germs around on their hands.

Speaking of hands, don't ever touch the handrails on stairs or escalators in the stations. The city recently conducted a survey, and reported most handrails have some sort of fecal matter on them. There is also no well-defined protocol for cleaning the railings. Those in the trains are cleaned at the end of the line, the railings in the stations, who knows if they ever receive a scrubbing. I've never seen anyone doing it, I've seen people mopping, picking up trash, but never cleaning a handrail.

The transit system will eventually be second nature and you'll know how to behave and where to transfer like a pro. You're one step closer to being a New Yorker. You'll use transit to save money, by taking the train out to meet friends on a Friday night. This works well until you're drunk and want to be home immediately, dropping twenty bucks on a cab to go half a mile. Oh well, you didn't move to the city to waste your time waiting for trains. Especially not when you need to get home to Netflix and order a grilled cheese and fries.

Once transit becomes familiar, the people in the train cars begin to piss you off. My friend Rebecca has the same pet peeve as many others: People who sit one seat in and leave the space closest to the door vacant. This means, a stranger is cuddled up to your side, while the space to their left is waiting vacant. This is the best seat on the train. Seriously, this is the seat people will shove past you to obtain, and this asshole is holding it hostage, daring someone to try and sit. Why do they do this? Honestly, I have no idea, I slide over the moment an end seat opens. You'll find all kinds of things to be annoyed by as you ride the train, guaranteed. Like when you swipe your MetroCard, pay your fare, and some kid after you jumps the turnstile. Little fucker.

The bus can also be a handy resource to assist in your travels, like the oh-so-popular walk of shame. You'll be taking that sexy bed head home early in the morning, and won't give two shits the man next to you is wearing a suit that costs as much as your rent. You have the memory of a great night out and almost good sex. If you're like me, the walk of shame happens at night as you don't spend the evening in a stranger's bed. You'll end up on the M15, just after sundown, only to realize there's jizz all over the front of your shirt. Does it matter? Probably, but no one cares enough to pay you mind, to even realize the shirt is wet. You feel like a sexy, slutty winner.

The train, the bus, really all forms of public transportation are your friends. Until someone throws up in a train car or a homeless person falls asleep. In these scenarios, transit is not your friend, and I recommend escaping the car as quickly as possible. Your New York nose can handle a lot of smells, but there's nothing like vomit and feces to put you off your night.

You'll only make the mistake once, or maybe twice, of entering an empty train car, when all of the other cars are packed full. The first time it happens you are filled with joy, thinking how lucky you are to be here at this moment, as the train rolls in and the car is full of seats for your tired ass. The doors open, you rush forward and a smell will slap you in the face. You gag, looking around for the source of the horrific stench that is destroying your soul. That's when you locate a man or woman, generally with large bags of stuff, probably all of their worldly possessions, huddled at one end of the train car. Sometimes asleep, sometimes chattering crazily, either way, the door has just closed and you can try to move between cars, which is technically illegal, or stick it out until the next stop. In the beginning, you will sympathize with this unfortunate soul, but once you catch the New York edge, you'll realize they have plenty of city-funded programs to help them get back on their feet.

If you think it's not illegal to move between the cars, ask my friend Disco Biscuits. Back when I worked at The Starting Line in Chelsea, which I'm sad to report recently closed its doors for good, I was waiting for him to arrive and open the store one Sunday morning. Twenty minutes late, I hate being forced to wait, he calls and tells me he needs me to come to the train station on 16th Street and 8th Avenue, to grab his bag because he's being arrested. I didn't believe him, but walked the two blocks only to find, he was in the station with two cops and in handcuffs. I laughed so hard, I nearly peed myself.

Turns out it's only a $50 ticket if you get caught passing between cars. The issue here was, Biscuits had an unpaid $75 ticket for peeing on the street. Also, [formerly] illegal, something I've been caught doing, but luckily not something which earned me a ticket. An unpaid ticket, plus a stop for a new citation, equates to an afternoon in the slammer.

Beware the empty train car, if no one is inside and it's not late at night, you probably don't want to be in there either.

6. Food

I'm not what one would call a "foodie." In fact, I'm probably one of the few people in the city who doesn't go to restaurants for the food a majority of the time. I do, however, go for the drinks and conversation. After drinks and good times, you eventually end up home, even if there's a stop at another person's home, we all get back to home base at some point. The slew of mobile apps which have exploded onto the scene, with all sorts of food gimmicks to lure you in, have become a trusted and important resource. You can order food, play a game and earn more free food, it's a win-win for your tummy.

From the back of a cab, you can order that grilled cheese and waffle fries, which make you want to kill yourself the next morning, but also fill your soul with joy in this one moment. There's a pattern here when I mention food, if you haven't noticed. We all have our secret food behaviors, things we do that erase the hours spent in the gym with each delicious bite, but once intoxicated it's nearly impossible to resist these convenient pleasures. We know in the back of our minds we're undermining those painful workouts, creating a fat ass and filling in those hard-to-get ab lines. Honestly, it's hard to care when something delicious is in your mouth.

You may not start out ordering too often when you arrive in the city. Ramen Noodles will be your best friend as you're paying your dues and suffering through the internship that promises lots of experience, even though it isn't offering any financial compensation. Take advantage of any free food in your office break room by stuffing your pockets and bag full. There's no shame in saving money on food, it's overpriced and each trip to the grocery store makes you want to cry a little. If you don't think food is expensive, just wait until you have to invest in supplements for your gym routine. Vitamins, protein and other related products are something you can either give a small fortune for and get the gains you desire, or you can skip them and more or less, only tone and slim down that fried food filled body. Meaning you'll end up as skinny-fat, which is a thing, look at half the celebrities being featured on magazines today. I mean, the photos that haven't been published and retouched. If only someone could be on hand to touch up every photo taken. We'd all be force feeding ourselves as the camera snapped shots and the visual guy fixed our double chins and butt dimples.

At some point in your city life, you will find the financial stability we all pretend to have and take up the act of ordering. Usually people go a little crazy when they start getting used to the convenience of food delivery. That is until you start looking at your bank statement, only to realize you've dropped several hundred dollars in the last month at a diner which serves free coffee and $5 burgers. Wallet shock will force you to be mindful of when and where you allow yourself to place an order.

For me: The only places deserving of my business are those not charging a delivery fee, and have a minimum order price of no more than $10. Why so cheap you ask? Well, when places start asking you to spend $15 or $20 as a minimum, you begin to add drinks and desserts to the order. When you're eating fries and cheese, you really don't need a slice of cheesecake, even if it is the most delicious cheesecake in the entire city. No, that cheesecake can rot in hell, you aren't going to get fat for a piece of $8 cheesecake. Okay, you will break every now and again, splurging on the delicious cheesecake, wishing you had the gag reflex to vomit it up. Models and teenage girls really are the luckiest people in the world, flaunting their uncontrollable bulimia in front of us all.

There is a consequence of all this food delivery you may not have considered. Because we all want our food and we want it ten minutes ago, there are hundreds of delivery people on foot and on bike, going every which way across the city. Those on foot are of no concern, those on bikes are another story. Having once been run over by a bike messenger, I have a special dislike for people on bicycles. I'm not joking; I was crossing the street where the Brooklyn Bridge pours cars and bikes into Manhattan, when an asshole mowed me down in the crosswalk. I had the right of way and he should have stopped for the red light.

Delivery people, well, actually, almost all people on bikes, fail to obey any rules of the road. They demand to be treated as cars, but refuse to behave like cars. The pedal pushing people of our little metropolis ride on the sidewalks, ringing those obnoxious bells for us [the pedestrians who the sidewalks exist for] to move. Why exactly did the city invest in all the bike lanes when these dicks are still riding on the sidewalk? Seriously, I'd love to know.

It doesn't stop there; Bicyclist run red lights, ignore walk signs and scream at pedestrians who get too close to them. They are a class of asshole all their own. And it's only gotten worse because we are now not only dealing with the delivery boys, and people trying to save the world by not driving, now we have CitiBike. Sweet Jesus, please, please let CitiBike lose funding and be ripped from our narrow streets. These horrible public bikes not only take up space on the sidewalk and streets, but they've created a group of causal bicyclists who are even more unaware of the rules of the road, riding around like they own the whole damn city. Sometimes it takes every bit of energy to not pick up a stick and shove it through the spokes of their front tire. Nothing would provide greater joy than to watch one of these people being knocked off their plastic pedestals.

It's the kind of joy/laughter you have to try and hold back because strangers will think you're sick. It's like when a ten-year-old hits a rut in the sidewalk and flies off their scooter. You have a pang in your side as you swallow the laughter. If you let it out the parents will likely be up in your face. In reality, you're overjoyed the two-wheeled monster was just smacked down by the Universe.

Truly, there's nothing we can do about the bicycle problem at this point, it's gone from a contained issue with the food delivery industry to the preferred hipster transportation method. I have to admit; I can't fathom why anyone would ride a bike to work or any other event. You arrive sweaty in the summer, you're wet in the winter and during the two weeks of the year when temperatures are perfect, you're in the way of everyone who has the self-respect to walk.

Don't get all bent out of shape and argue we need bikes to reduce pollution and save the world. Ride the train like a normal person or start using a car share service. There are plenty of ways to reduce your carbon footprint without hopping on a bike and pissing all of us off. Yes, all of us are angry at you, not just the five voices in my head. It makes no sense, I mean, if you want to help save the planet, start by getting on board with the reality that we live in a train and bus driven city.

Back on the topic of food. Delivery is your best friend and enemy, be careful and cultivate your relationship wisely. On the flip side, be extra cautious when it comes to going out to dinner. It's amazing how often the bill will be several hundred dollars. If you're pinching pennies, find an excuse to meet up with friends after they've finished dinner. That, or be like me and flat out say you'll meet them after dinner because you don't want to eat at wherever they're going. New York City is full of fantastic restaurants and all of them have fantastic wine and cocktail lists. You may only order an appetizer, but the four bottles of wine are going to cost a small fortune. When it comes to splitting bills you'll find yourself paying for more than your fair share, it's just how things shake out. After all, you don't want to be the cheap, asshole friend who throws a tantrum over fifty bucks. Though that fifty bucks is going to be the difference between a fun night with friends and eating for the next week.

This idea of penny pinching regarding food is also worth keeping in mind as you date, don't let dates take you out to dinner. Unless you're a straight female, then totally go out to dinner, society says the guy has to and will pay for your meal. If you're a gay man or women, it's pretty common to split the check. Make sure your date is happening over coffee or drinks, even better, make a suggestion as to where this date can take place. Most people hate picking the location, but if you make the suggestion it's much easier to control the outcome of the bill and contain your food related expenses.

7. Creepy Crawlers

The entirety of my life has *not* been spent in a city proper. Until the age of twelve we, my family and I, lived in and around Salt Lake City, Utah, eventually my father's wife of the time declared she was unable to live under the oppressive smog of the city. Thus, we moved to the middle of nowhere. *Literally.*

Hoystville, Utah: [Insert lifeless facial expression here.] A town which only has a sign to signify its existence on the expressway because my grandfather worked for the Highway Commission for much of his post-war career. It was erected as a part of his retirement...a poetic gift I suppose. Both of my father's parents grew up in this blip of a town. Most people in this place have farms and animals, the air is clean and it's the type of town which will bore a person to death.

That came off as a dig on my grandparents, not the intention. They're the type of people you would expect to come from such a wholesome place. Honest, hardworking, religious people, who are unusually kind to every man, woman and child.

Perhaps a person is only able to turn out as described if born into small town life. I spent seven years living in the same small town and turned out rather different. I ramble because I'm no stranger to the creepy crawlers of the country, illustrating my point in the most longwinded of ways possible. New York is not the country... well, maybe parts of Staten Island count as country, but for this point we will exclude Staten Island. This and every other point I try to make.

Have you ever seen a water bug up close and personal? In the city, people will tell you cockroaches are water bugs. They do love water and all things clean or dirty, but not all nasty, brown bugs with wings are water bugs. When they're an inch or three long these nasty things are usually cockroaches. Water bugs do exist and you'll run into them now and again in the bathroom or near the kitchen sink. They're quick little things which will make you jump as they always appear unexpectedly. They usually aren't too big and really are no cause for alarm. Gross, but not dangerous.

Brooklyn was where I first made the unfortunate acquaintance with cockroaches. Not in the first apartment, but in the second. My roommate, Lacee, and I were living in the slanted building as previously mentioned and seeing as it was old and unkept there were plenty of things inside the walls. You can learn to tolerate these monsters because there's no other choice. I can only imagine the horror of renovating an old building and seeing all the gross shit living inside the walls. Best to kill what crawls out and not ponder what lives just beyond sight.

It's even possible to learn to tolerate mice. The first time a mouse made itself known was when a glue trap, accidentally left behind a newly installed dishwasher, did its job too effectively and caught a four-legged fiend. But, it wasn't immediately obvious to Lacee and I that anything had been caught. A few weeks after the mouse was trapped in glue, a terrible odor hung in the air all around the kitchen. We searched the cabinets for rotting food, cleaned out the fridge, scrubbed everywhere we could think. Eventually we recalled there had been a glue trap sitting where the dishwasher now lived. The machine was nothing but a hole when we moved in, the occasional, furry gray mouse darting out from behind the cabinets. One building super, one power drill and one decomposing mouse later the apartment was stink free. Though the sight of the rotting mouse will forever stick in the back of my head along with that wretched smell.

These are the things which you grow to love, *in a sense*, because they're shoved in your face at every turn. Rats in the subway, possum sized rats in the streets of Brooklyn at night. By the way, these rats are scary as all hell, and I can personally attest to the fact that they will hiss and spit at you. Seriously, they are enormous and should be left alone. If you don't believe me, just lift a trash can lid every now and again as you wander the streets, you'll find one of these huge beasts feasting on trash.

There is one particular creature that roams apartments in the dark hours of the night. One creature, which if you admit to having in your apartment will cause any New Yorker to back away from you in absolute horror. One creature which is nearly impossible to kill: The Bed Bug. *Cue dramatic, scary music.*

Now, I already mentioned the fact we experienced bed bugs. But let's dig a little deeper into the story. There was a period of four days where I barely slept. The kitchen table was pulled into the center of the kitchen, where I would rest on top with no blanket in an effort to stay bite free. The myth about bed bugs is that they only live in your bed. This is the biggest lie you've ever been told. I mean, biggest lie not involving a government cover up. I have a friend who will do his damnedest to tell you 9/11 was an inside job. We disagree, but you get the point.

Bed bugs enjoy being in your bed because you are the food source. They also like living in your closet because the skin cells you shed onto clothing attract them. This is why it can be so stressful to have them, they will get you no matter where you try and hide. Oh, and if you're wondering how they find and bite you, it's the carbon dioxide you breathe out which they are able to detect with their little bug sensors. In order to avoid the bites, stop breathing, it's really that simple.

Once the bugs are gone you will never forget or feel a true sense of relief. Two years later while I was living in a studio on the Upper East Side the bites started once more. I tried to tell myself it was nothing more than mosquitos and ignored the issue. Well, wouldn't you know, plain as day, I saw one of the little jerks crawling up the wall. Taping it to the wall as proof, I summoned the management company. They called Roscoe, this cute beagle seen on television, who can sniff out bed bugs. Yep, they had come back to get me; Bed Bugs the Sequel!

It turns out the source of these bed bugs, mind you we still don't know where those in our Brooklyn apartment came from officially, were from the second floor of the building. One apartment was riddled with them and they spread throughout the building when the occupant moved. It took several months and the same painful checklist of life deconstructing tasks to get rid of them. To this day, if I get a bite from anything while inside an apartment, panic sets in and I begin to scratch and search. Search for signs of bed bugs, knowing they have come back to finish me off as one would expect of Act III in any poorly produced play.

The place I live now, also on the Upper East Side, has mosquitos due to a construction site on the adjacent lot. They get in through the air conditioner vents, I assume, and feast during the night. Deet is my best friend after a shower and before bed.

Let this be a lesson, there is no escaping the bugs of New York City. No matter the cost of rent or stature of the neighborhood, they're here to stay and you better learn to tolerate our tiny friends. If you're like me and douching yourself with bug spray, it also helps to pray the stuff won't cause cancer ten years down the road. Fingers crossed.

8. Hooking Up

Actually making the decision and executing on the move to New York will feel like the hardest thing anyone has ever done. That is, until you actually begin living in the city. It won't take long before you realize how expensive the world is and how truly poor you are. You may do as Lacee and I did while we were rooming together and eat spaghetti-o's from a can in the dark, because your building has no power in the middle of a horrific summer heatwave. Another option is to live off of the high-sodium, Ramen Noodles, sold for a quarter in most bodegas. I've eaten my weight in chicken flavored ramen. If the sodium didn't do any long-term damage to my organs it will be a miracle.

Yes, your cuisine will be simple and a necessary sacrifice as you are working to establish an existence in this big, beautiful place. Getting by is made easier as long as you stay in the apartment and avoid luxuries like coffee, alcohol and fun in general. This will suddenly be made even more of difficult a task, saving and staying in, when you are asked out for the first time.

There's an assumption here that you, the reader, have been on a date before in life and this is not your first adventure. This will be your first New York City date; to which we are referring. Your date, likely met from one of the many options available on your sexy, little smartphone, will be perfect. You'll obsess over the person's profile, stalk them via social channels and realize they're much more of a New Yorker than you. Worth noting, even after you have become a true city dweller you'll behave this way, it's just what people do these days.

Here's where the panic sets in for the upcoming date. The person probably isn't a native, they usually avoid anyone who smells new to the big apple. Like a disease, the jaded native will keep clear of newbies. Your date is most likely also a transplant from somewhere out West or down South, isn't it fun how these old sayings have stuck around, who has lived here for three, five or eight years. Where am I getting these numbers? Personal experience, your experience may differ in numbers and a thousand other ways.

So, you go out on the date, doing everything possible to avoid looking like a moron. Intellectually you're safe, you've obtained a college degree, which put you in debt and now collects dust as you work a crap job that required a degree to apply, but your degree doesn't apply to anything you do at this job. Different subject, but it really is insane what companies demand of employees as far as education. The fear here is the person across the table will realize you've only been in the city a few short months. God forbid this revelation come to light before they fall madly in love with you, allowing him/her to make the kind decision of overlooking your poor decision to not move here sooner.

The date talks about this bar on the Lower East Side, a great museum on the Upper East Side, some pub in Midtown and a cool art installation in the Financial District. You sip on a twelve-dollar drink, hoping you're not expected to pay, nodding your head and agreeing with every word coming your direction. Sure, you know the one place he/she mentioned. Hell yes, you love that museum and you've seen the whatever-art-it-is twice already.

In reality, you're scratching your head, some of the guys may be scratching their balls, it just works that way some times, as you have never heard of any of these things. Where's NoHo and did the person across from you just say FiDi? Are these real places or have you just awoken to find yourself in some twisted reality show where everything is spoken in shorthand?

Not only are you on a date, you're also sitting through an educational seminar regarding New York City and what makes it a hip, cool place. One verbal faux pas and your date will know you have no clue about the city, and that you still get lost half the time when exiting a subway station. This is not a dramatization; people will walk out on you if the date is going poorly. Not everyone is a nice person when it comes to love, dating and sex. Some of them may be nice and give you an excuse as to why they have to leave, but there's also the chance they won't be there when you come back from the bathroom. No one is able to handle uncomfortable moments in our over-connected and under-socialized bubble. It's better to flee the situation as quietly as possible, in their minds.

There's no way for me to predict the actual outcome of your date. If I attempt to do so I would be a Madame Cleo sized fraud. *Can I be sued for that comment?* You may go home with this person and enjoy your first NYC walk of shame. Which is a chapter unto itself in the book of me. Though one of my favorites is worth sharing before we leave the world of dating.

There was this guy I'd been crushing on, who was friends with someone I went on a couple dates with before realizing it wasn't worth the time. Anyway, being incredibly nervous on the date, I became beyond drunk, was handcuffed (by my date), fucked incredibly hard and then allowed to pass out drunk on his friend's pullout bed as he was visiting from London. So, of course this all happened at his friend's house.

This is just bragging; the part I find comical is three hours later when he woke me up to kick my ass out. I dressed and did my best to slip out without making much noise. In the elevator I realized I was going to vomit, but there was a lady in there with me and too many people outside. It was the crack of dawn on a Saturday, does no one sleep in these days?

How was I going to puke without making a scene? Heading back upstairs, I knocked on the door and politely asked to use the bathroom. The date and his friend heard me wretch my guts out before coming out with a large smile and heading home. To survive here one must leave all shame in the past. Plus, when you really need to use the bathroom, from either end, who really cares if someone can hear. They should be polite, and less gross, and not listen.

Perhaps you and your date will share a pleasant goodnight kiss and never speak again, or even go on to have several more dates before a pregnancy scare which inevitably rips you apart and leaves you broken and bitter. Wear those battles wounds with honor because the more scars you have, the better you are at surviving within this concrete jungle. Just remember to use a condom. I emphasize this message to all of my lady friends who have no kids, let's keep it that way and make sure the boys are bagging up.

I share this here, as dating gets easier the longer you live in the city. Dating doesn't necessarily get better the longer you're here, but it does get significantly easier. The first year dating is problematic because you often are choosing between food and shelter or a date. Unless you are Taylor Swift and moving here with tons of money. See how I took it back to my main point? I bet Taylor never has dates walk out on her, or has to live in slanted apartments with bed bugs. But it would be awesome if she came to visit! Roommates are not only a necessity for new residents, but they can also provide much needed human contact as you consciously make an effort to not go outside to avoid the expense. Roommates are sort of like a live-in boyfriend/girlfriend, whom you are not obligated to fuck, pays half the rent, eats your food and listens to your bullshit dating stories.

As you become more familiar with whichever neighborhood you call home and begin to explore others, you'll learn where all the best dollar pizza joints are located, and where to go for three-dollar vodka and beers during happy hour. Dating simply becomes a trick of guiding the situation to places you know inside out, and hopefully a few watering holes where you've got a friend behind the bar to help you save a few bucks.

A rookie mistake we all make is letting the date define the where just because they know more places. This is when you get stuck with splitting those big bills we want to avoid. Going Dutch is so common on a date in this city, you should sleep with anyone who flat out buys you dinner. I'm serious, and this doesn't qualify as prostitution, it's how you give a proper thank you and ensure it happens a second time. Remember, you're poor and anyone who wants to give out a free meal without requiring you to stand in line is awesome.

To be completely up front, in my humble, yet often arrogant, opinion, anyone living in New York for less than two years is better off having hookups instead of trying to find a boyfriend/girlfriend. Aside from the fact casual sex can be pleasurable and exciting, it saves you from missing out on important experiences. It's rare to find someone who says, "I love exploring the city," and backs the sentiment up with action. Often, this translates into one or two walks around the park and devolves into Netflix marathons. I'm all for binge watching now and then, but you're in the most exciting city in the world. There is no reason to tie yourself to someone so early on and miss out on the fun.

People are going to disagree with me here, as usual, especially the people who are currently in long-term relationships. To those people, fuck off. Relationship people are the first to ask why you're single, make you feel bad for not being in a committed relationship and are usually some of the biggest douche bags. Take comfort in knowing these people also get married too fast, divorced quickly and are usually saddled with multiple children before their thirtieth birthday. There are a few relationship people out there who are down-to-earth, awesome people, they are as rare as Bigfoot and even harder to find. Ignore the advice of people in relationships, this is my point, they are just as clueless as you when it comes to dating. Wouldn't it be funny if I was in a serious relationship whenever this book is released and was forced to eat my words? Won't happen, but it would be comical.

Play the field for a while when you arrive. Have a date on the waterfront in Brooklyn, take another date to a movie in Central Park during the summer, go ice skating in Bryant Park and enjoy all the things around you. Download one of the hookup apps if for no other reason than to see random pictures of stranger's penises. I promise, male or female, guys will eagerly send you dick pics, even if not explicitly requested. You can have a good laugh with friends at this person's expense without them ever knowing. If you like what you see, have a sexy little fling. Wrap it up and enjoy.

I say all of this having recently had this conversation in a bar after a stranger walked up to me:

"You here alone?"
"No."
"Are you single?"

"Yes."

"Why?"

"What do you mean?"

"Don't you want a boyfriend?"

"No."

Silence. Then the person walked away from me. Is it so unbelievable to think some people don't want a relationship? You are thinking I'm just a bitter twat who doesn't know what he's talking about. You're right to a degree, I'm super bitter, but it's not because anyone hurt me or emotionally cut me, it's because I'm bitter and it tastes good. Some people are good at things others are not, I'm terrible at being in relationships. I am selfish, independent and don't like to share my bed, space or anything else.

On the other hand, this is not to say being alone is the goal. Something about people who need people are the luckiest people kind of bullshit. I need people: Friends. Friends can fulfill all of your emotional needs while staying far enough away to give you space. A fuck buddy can take care of everything else.

My fuck buddy has actually become one of my favorite people. He's a few years older, not as neurotic and a pretty nice guy. In short, a few times a year, I come and go, literally. That is more than enough in my book. Yes, there was a point I was gross and desperate and wanted to try and lock said fuck buddy down in a relationship. In hindsight, it seems this was more about someone telling me I couldn't do something. No is not something I do all too well.

Finding a fuck buddy can be a little difficult as you're not going to have a conversation when you first meet someone and agree to be their regular hook up. It happens on its own, unless you're a hooker, then you're everybody's fuck buddy. It likely will take you a few years to find this person, but they'll come along if you're out of a relationship long enough. When you're in an out of relationships with frequency, it's like you catch some sort of odor others can detect and learn to avoid. Just one person's opinion.

9. I Spy

Voyeurism is the sexual interest in watching or spying on other people. Living in almost any city, it's a sport, often with very little sex appeal. It may be your preference to causally people watch like a Parisian from the comfort of a cafe while mocking those who pass by with your friends. Or, you may be blatant, loud-mouthed-assholes like my friends and I. We have no qualms about judging those, out loud, as they pass. I have to admit, there have even been photos taken and spread via social media. Yes, it's true, we are kind of assholes. But the fun kind of assholes. Aside from one social incident where a photo was captioned 'everlasting Gobstopper' usually it's well received as the joke the mocking is intended to be, not cyberbullying as some say. There are however more uptight, politically correct people in the modern world and nothing makes them happier than ruining everyone's fun.

Watching others isn't really a sexual thing in my case, it's just good old fashioned fun at the expense of another who has no idea...which is a big part of what makes the watching fun. With buildings all around and windows so close to one another, it's almost impossible to not watch your neighbors. If you can avoid watching, you have the willpower of a saint and deserve some sort of award.

The first person I became fascinated with watching was a woman living across the air shaft and down a level. Her kitchen window always had the shades up and she was usually walking around, always dressed, so don't get too worried about the pervert factor. There was never a point where I saw her face because my view was on a downward slant and only gave view from her shoulders down. It became habit to stare down into her window as I fixed breakfast or snacked during the day. Across the Shaft Lady often reorganized her cabinets. An act which seems odd when you only have two of them. She would drag her pots, pans, bowls, etc. out and stack everything upon the table and then pile it all back into the cabinets in a slightly different arrangement. Not insane but odd to say the least because it was happening more than once a week.

This was only the first taste in my obsessive joy taken from peeping at people. Once on the Upper East Side, 84th Street to be exact, there were an array of people coming and going. The restaurant on the corner, directly across from my window, was a popular and longstanding establishment, drawing the college crowd. As I was informed, by my mother of all people when she recognized the restaurant's name, in the 1980's some rich, college dude left with a girl, raped and murdered her in Central Park. So, think of this, one minute you may be creeping on someone who could potentially be tomorrow's breaking news.

St. Patrick's Day, 2012, sitting with my mom and two beers on the fire escape, drunks are wandering around like ants at street level. One fat, white man is beyond trashed. Appearing to be alone, he does his best to entertain onlookers as he climbs atop the hood of a police car, doing a sexy, pinup pose. This was probably the most hysterical drunk moment to which I have ever been witness and not involved. The impressive moment was when the cops returned and instead of busting the drunk or ticketing him, they simply laughed, coaxed him off the vehicle and returned him to the safety of the sidewalk before leaving.

The cops may have left, but that didn't mean Mr. Drunk was ready to call it a day. No, he unzipped, took a piss on a mailbox and then walked up to the unsuspecting bouncer of the bar to shake his hand. We shouted from the fire escape in a fit of laughter, trying to warn the bouncer that he'd just grabbed a filthy hand covered in urine. Our cries went unheard and eventually drunky stumbled into the street. Now it became a watch and wait game to see if he'd fall or actually hail a cab. In this city, cab drivers discriminate against drunks. If you are visibly intoxicated, it's not uncommon to have great trouble finding a cab, mainly because they don't want your vomit on their seats. Seems fair.

Standing in the middle of the intersection, cabs slowed before seeing the drunk man stumble towards them, only to speed away. He fell only once, rebounding as the girls on the street glared in disgust. Unfortunately, like all good stories, it ended too soon as he wandered up the street and out of sight. I assume the man made it home as I didn't hear anything on the news the following day, reporting on a man found dead in a puddle of ale flavored vomit.

On the same street, one summer, late in the evening I was in bed when a screaming and pounding started. Ignoring it for a moment in the vain hope whomever was causing the ruckus would shut up or go away, I was forced to look out the window as the noise continued. At the door of the building across the street stood a bulky man. Slamming his fist on the buzzer pad, it was my guess someone was intentionally ignoring him. He then began screaming obscenities and kicking the glass door.

This continued and without warning, though the result should have been expected, the glass door fractured in frame. It looked one touch away from falling to the ground in a million sharp little pieces. The man realized what he'd done and rushed back into the bar next door, the same bar mentioned a moment ago where the girl was taken from and murdered, though there is no connection between the two events. If breaking the door wasn't a big enough mistake, the second mistake came two minutes later when the psycho emerged from the bar just as a pissed off Italian guy in his boxers came flying out of the building, the one which was just being hammered with a fist.

Now, I'm pretty sure these men have never met and the only reason we have the angry Italian appearing is because it's likely his apartment was being buzzed when this guy was banging on the keypad. The newcomer assessed the door and looked at the screamer who was now dead silent. The words were inaudible, but it looked from the hand gestures as if the Italian was asking if the guy broke the door. Waving his hands, the man clearly lied, knowing this other dude could probably fuck him up.

Moral of the story: If you're going to be an asshole, especially one who damages property and disturbs people who are trying to sleep, make sure there are no Italians living nearby, they won't stand for your shit. Also, be a man and confess you're the asshole who did the dirty deed. Nothing worse than an asshole who is also a pussy.

These are a few random stories to explain what it means to people watch from the comfort of your home. You'll see a million crazy people in broad daylight just as interesting. When I first arrived on this tiny island, I sat on a SoHo street eating lunch, when a man walked by in nothing but a purple thong and his long black hair braided into two lengthy pigtails. He is the most confident person I've ever encountered, and is probably still wandering the streets of SoHo just looking for people to shock.

It takes a lot to shock a person the longer they live in New York, but from day one you should be observing and absorbing the sights and sounds around you. For the writers, it's fuel for your blogs and books, and for everyone else it's the funny story you'll have at the next party when trying to impress people. Remember, every story is worth sharing, even if you need to spice it up a little. For example, who says the purple thong man couldn't have been completely naked? Stranger sightings have occurred.

10. Run Far Away

New York can wear on you. When you arrive in the bright eyed phase of your life, it's hard to imagine ever growing weary of the glowing lights. To my horror, I was actually warned of this one afternoon in early Fall. I was exiting the Starbucks located on the Southeast corner of Union Square. I distinguish only because there is another Starbucks on the Northwest corner. Both have horrifically long lines, no seating and tons of obnoxious tourists. Tourists: *Hiss!* [Note: After writing this, it came to my attention Starbucks not only remodeled the NW location, but moved a block South. The lines inside remain unchanged.]

This particular afternoon, as I exited with my skinny vanilla latte in hand, a homeless, or what I assumed to be a homeless, man appeared from seemingly nowhere. Now, he may have just been dressed in dirty, dingy clothing, this is a stereotype, but as so many of these are true, I'm going to let it ride and conclude this individual made his nightly home on a park bench.

So, here I come walking out, feeling cock-of-the-walk confident as I'm conquering the city in my naive head. Then he blurts,

"I used to be young and pretty like you. Get out of this city while you can, before you're wrinkled and gray."

Momentarily stunned, I walked away thinking, this guy said, *'I'm young and pretty,'* how awesome am I? It took several years before his message began to resonate. Around twenty-five the hair on my chin started to turn white. In fact, all the hair, only on my chin, has turned white. It looks like I've been cum splattered and didn't have the sense to clean myself up. This is why we never grow out the facial hair. #PersonalProblems

Then around twenty-eight, I noticed the worry wrinkle appearing on my forehead. In all honesty, wrinkles should have started showing on my face around twenty-two. As a Virgo, everything is a big deal, work is the ultimate form of stress and tormenting one's self is how we Virgos deal with any and everything.

I've thought about the homeless guy's warning in the past few years and wondered if he was right. Should the young and pretty people run screaming from New York, long before the city can rape their faces through experiences? **NO!** I mean, get out of the city now and again, just because we all need a reminder of the fools who don't live in this magical place. Do not avoid living in the city because you're afraid of a few wrinkles and color changing hairs.

This place is going to rape your face and every other part of your body. Sometimes it's going to be wretched, financially devastating and seemingly impossible to withstand. This is why there is some cheap food on the bottom of bodega shelves, places to hangout on every block so you can avoid cab and transit fare, and people who will befriend you for being a badass who doesn't give in when things get rough.

Don't get me wrong, I'm not changing my cynical tune and telling you it's all positive from here on out. That's not my style and at this point, I feel you would be disappointed in me for doing so. In the spirit of the chapter, let's go through some random fucked up things that have happened to me and the souls who collect near and around me.

Lacee, my roommate of years gone by, and I went to this gay dance bar, The Ritz. It's the best you can get when looking for a dance floor that's just the right amount of sticky, sweaty and slutty. We sat ourselves out front with the smokers for a dance break, just as the drag queen with Jell-O shots passed by asking if anyone was buying. We purchased and the drag queen leaned in to say,

"Your makeup looks so good; you almost look like a real woman."

Lacee wanted to die, I spit my blue Jell-O shot all over her jeans in a fit of laughter and the drag queen traipsed away. Moral of the story: As a well-kept/groomed lady, it's possible people will confuse you with being a man when in a gay club. This is either an ego blow or a compliment, your choice.

Not bad enough? Okay, have you ever seen on television or in person the metal doors in the sidewalk which lead to building basements? If you watched Sex and the City, you'll know Samantha once fell into one and had to wear a boot on her foot as a toe healed. I was leaving my friend Larrymore's birthday in Astoria when my drunk ass walked over one. As a regular over consumer of alcohol, walking is not always my specialty. On this particular night in October of 2014 the odds were fully stacked against me. I stepped on the closed doors and inward one went, taking with it my foot. Moving at the speed of New York, my walking pace is rather fast. My full face slapped the concrete so hard I was momentarily stunned.

A girl picked up my glasses, handing them back to me as I shooed her away and scuttled off. Making my way to the train, I only realized something was wrong when people began to stare. Flipping the phone into selfie mode, I glanced at my face. The entire right side of my face was covered in fresh, shiny blood.

The next day I felt the pain in my face, shoulder and shin, the scars are still visible to prove the story true and I now step more lightly over those metal doors to hell.

Maybe you prefer a little pain over humiliation. I have two New York tattoos, one of which is the Brooklyn Bridge. People ask me: *Why?* For the love of god, why would you dig this into your flesh? Because, you dick. That's why. But honestly, I love Brooklyn. That place beat the shit out of me, and if that's something I can survive, then nothing is going to take me down. Except maybe an STD...something to ponder. So, I etched the bridge into my tit.

Laying back in the chair of the tattoo artist, the owner was shuffling around with her cell phone. Then, almost ready to cry because I'm a baby, and bleeding because someone is digging into my flesh, the owner stands over me and begins taking photos. *Click. Click. Click.* I'm pretty sure my pasty, bloody, crybaby ass ended up on their Facebook page. It's like the first time you have sex and the dude is recording and then you discover it's been posted to Vine. I say Vine because most people only last a few seconds the first time. At least if it was a sex tape, I'd get famous and have my own douche bag reality show. Alas, it was just tattoos, tears and one scary old lady documenting my pain.

Still not good enough? How about your drug dealer meeting your mom? Okay, to preface, I'm not a junkie or anything crazy, but the occasional drug use is ubiquitous with being a New Yorker. We all do it now and then and it's just easier to have someone on speed dial than to hit up friends and strangers. Plus, it's impossible to be sure your friends are packing when you decide you want a little somethin'. Much more convenient to have your own connection. However, this can turn you into a drug dealer of sorts, because once your friends know you have a connection they come to you to use it with frequency.

Mom was in the city for my twenty-sixth birthday and we went to my favorite, now defunct, dive, View Bar. A dingy, shit hole of a place with nice, old guys who don't bother you. My dealer made deliveries back then because she wasn't as popular. Sometimes I wish we could go back to those days, such a simpler time. She shows up, brings her stuff and then starts talking to my mother. I'm shitting my pants. This is like the ultimate setup for a parental crackdown.

To my surprise, mom never knew this was anyone other than a friend, and today, even though mom is long gone, God rest her soul, if you believe in a god, my dealer still brings her up. Seriously, every single time I see my dealer she talks about mom. She also talks about how my sister is a cunt, but that's a story for another book, it's called Bulletproof, look it up. And yes, I still do drugs on occasion and have a dealer. In fact, she's my longest running, successful relationship.

I can tell, you're still not feeling like I've given you enough gritty, city dirt. Queens, holes, drugs, what will it take to please you? Would the time I was thrown out of a bar for giving a lap dance and refusing to pull my pants up do the trick? No, that happened in Philly. Maybe a threesome, one of the people being the brother of a guy who was a dick to me in high school. Nah, that's just karma. Perhaps the boyfriend of an ex who cheated, looking me up for a hookup. Lord no, that's just slutty and gross. A drunken rampage in Brooklyn ending with getting lost and not being able to find a cab home? Still no.

I think the winner of horror stories goes to my good friend Brittany. At another bar which no longer exists, at least in the location which it once did, Joshua Tree, we sat for drinks. After getting properly drunk we both danced on the bar, I was thrown off because guys can't do such things in a straight bar. Brit then tossed a drink in the bartender's face because he wouldn't flirt with her. Then, she passed out on the toilet with her panties down, followed by the waitress sending me in to fetch her because the cops were out front. I don't know why the cops were there, but they were and it freaked my ass out.

My hot mess friend [now mostly reformed], whom I love, then wobbled as I propped her against a tree and tried hailing a cab. This is not the same time I lectured her over drinking, but gives an example of how our drinking plays out. Yes, I lectured someone on drinking, which in itself is the biggest, scariest oxymoron in the universe. In the end, we always have a good time, though the older we get the more of our good times seem to be happening on a sofa with a bottle of wine.

New York will age you, the homeless man was right about that. You're going to be worn down and out like a ten-dollar hooker working a Queens corner every weekend for a decade. Hookers at the Point, watch it, this is your life with fewer cameras but more flashing. And it's worth all the effort, vomiting, tears and fun.

11. Terrible Two

It is my personal belief that if you can survive the first two years of life in New York, you can survive just about anything that's thrown your way. More important, if you can survive the first two years, it's likely you won't puss out, pack up and move back home. It takes two to make or break you. At least, that's what I've seen time and again with newbies who attempt to call our city home.

Lacee, who I've been referencing like my personal word slave, made it past the two-year mark. She is one of the exceptions to my rule. She didn't technically puss out and go home, she caught a case of the pregnancy and didn't want to deal with strollers, subways, stairs and crowds. Can't blame her there, I mean, children and city life don't really mix.

Have you ever gone to a restaurant where your meal costs several hundred dollars and there was a child screaming as you're trying to enjoy a nice glass of wine and a piece of meat? Unacceptable. Depending on your personality, the meat you're enjoying could be a dick under the table or a steak, either way it always ends up costing a few hundred bucks. Damn, I should give up this writing thing and become a hooker.

"If I had a nickel for every time I've given it away for free, I'd be independently, fucking wealthy."

True statement, from my mother's mouth to these pages. Anyway, this chapter is not meant to be about sucking dick. Though to be honest, in your first two years, especially if you're a gay guy coming from a small town, you'll probably suck a lot of dick. Case and point, me, [I apologize to my future self for writing this] my number of sexual partners was relatively low the day I arrived in New York City. In the low twenties, and by the time I'd reached my second year in the city, I'd more than doubled the number. Mind you the first twenty-something took place over seven years. You do the dirty math, that's a lot of dick for one mouth to handle. This is purely to illustrate the point, believe me this isn't worth bragging about...it would be great if some of these guys could be erased from my mind, mouth and soul.

It's not just your mouth, like Lacee, you may take a semen shot to the vag every now and again. This is why you should double bag your business, you never know when a super swimmer will make an appearance and transform [ruin] your adult life. So, Lacee moved back to Utah, where she still resides and I await the day when she returns to the real world. Though, when she does come back, she best be rich, she's going to need a nanny to watch the two kids while we're out drinking and gallivanting. Brunch and babies do not mix.

Survival goes beyond the stress of finding a decent apartment, hooking up with guys/girls, and affording food. Friendship in the city is cyclical. See, I told you we were going to circle back to this topic. For reasons or forces which seem to be beyond the control of any one person, friendships tend to peak every two years. The friends I first made when living in Brooklyn faded away as our lives moved in different directions and to different neighborhoods. Some came back after a few years, while others were replaced. Some friends faded away as calls and text messages became less frequent, while others disagreed with the personal choices I made and turned away.

It will only be a small core group of people who stick by your side. What surprised me were the people who walked away willingly. I value friendships more than romantic relationships. One is filled with drama and strings where the other is built upon mutual interests. You can determine which you want to be which as for me the latter is friendship. Those likeminded people who you find and befriend are worth fighting to keep.

Animator, a close friend who has faded in and out, being forgotten by mutual friends for his flakiness, is one friend I cling to, even though a year or more sometimes passes between seeing one another. Why keep a friend who is never around and often cancels plans? Because we all have shit going on, if you're going to be so sensitive and controlling, maybe you don't deserve the people you call friends. **Don't be a dick friend.**

So, what are the things to think about when trying to survive the first two years you may ask. Again, this is all from my selfish perspective, other people I'm sure will disagree and they can write their own books to do so. I say the first thing you must do is erase all images from your mind of the television, imagined, New York lifestyle. Giant apartments for twenty-somethings who wait tables aren't a reality. Unless you actually are sucking a lot of dick or spending the night with your daddy. You will be poor and living in a tiny space, sometimes with two to five people. There are many newbies who cram far more people into one expensive apartment to make it work.

Friendship. Find the weirdos you can relate to and lock them down. It can be difficult, but if you connect with someone, put in the time and energy to make a friendship work. Living in this place is much easier when there are people you can count on and crack open a bottle of wine to share. **Don't confuse friendship and dating.** Even if you have a steady someone, you need friends, if for no other reason than to bitch about the person you're dating.

The two-year cycle impacts more than friendships, this is just one area where it is very easy to see the change. I believe the reason these changes occur is because, like a Taylor Swift album, we drastically change every two years. We may work the same jobs and have the same habits, but a lot takes place over two years.

In two years, you begin loving places you've never been, hate the places which were once your favorite, notice the generation gap between you and the 'kids today.' Everything changes over and over, but because it happens in these two year stretches it can be easy to miss. You may not notice that moving from Brooklyn into Manhattan will change your course, uproot friendships and cut you off from things you love. While at the same time a friend(s) moving from Manhattan to Jersey City, may be killing you inside because you're not prepared to allow change. It's all going to happen and there's nothing you can do.

Life is like your hair, you have to wash, drink and repeat.

12. Booze

I've never met a single person in New York who didn't drink. This is not to say everyone is a drunk, alcoholic, booze-hound...whatever your terminology. For those who abstain from the liquid pleasure, be it choice or religious imprisonment, it's going to be difficult to take in all this big, bright city has to offer when you're saying "no" to happy hour.

Start with the workplace. How many deals are made over cocktails? Be it lunch or after work, you're going to bond with colleagues and business partners over drinks. The clink of the glass is the beginning and end of most careers. I'm living proof of this concept. A majority of my career has evolved through conversations which took place at dinner with the assistance of two or more bottles of wine. Always two because one is for me and the other is for the rest of the table.

Alcohol extends all the way from work relationships to friendships. You may start as some random, lonely single in a bar, desperately trying to meet your next great love or perhaps your new best friend, but if you aren't drinking, no one is going to give you the time of day. The sober person to a real New Yorker is unnerving. Not necessarily because you aren't/don't drink, but because most people who aren't drinking in a bar or restaurant have some sort of hidden agenda to push. Be you an activist, a religious zealot or something other, we don't want to engage in a conversation with someone who is likely to throw a drink in our face when they discover we don't agree with whatever bullshit they are peddling. That would be an offensive waste of good alcohol.

All that being out on the table, New Yorkers love brunch. It's not just a way of life, it's a sport. If you don't believe me, the next time you're out on a Sunday afternoon, try telling someone there is no unlimited brunch at the restaurant they're in line for. They'll either walk away and find a new establishment which caters to their desire for ninety minutes of pleasure, or they'll respond, "*Are you fuckin' kiddin' me?*"

What's so special about brunch? For most of the United States, brunch simply means eggs after 11:00 am. In New York City, it means that as well, but it also means your booze comes with the meal and you can drink all day long, judgement free. If you are like my group of friends, you search for the perfect brunch spot all week long before committing to a reservation. Yes, you want to make sure you've made a reservation or you're in for a long, long wait.

Most restaurants give you somewhere between one and two hours to drink your choice of mimosas, bloodies and now and again vodka sodas. You do need to be on point with your game when it comes to how the unlimited works for each restaurant. Does the timing begin when they take the order or serve the drink? Confirm the actual time the waiter or waitress has noted as your start time. It's not uncommon for the restaurant to not tell you when your unlimited period has ended. Pay attention to the clock or you'll probably have a handful of full-priced drinks on the bill, negating the entire brunch purpose.

It's also wise to avoid places that only serve unlimited while you're eating. This means you have to eat like a high school cheerleader, itty bitty bites, a difficult task once the alcohol begins to hit, and all you want is to shove a pancake in your mouth while chugging a fist full of mimosa goodness. A tip from me to you, downtown there is a delicious French bistro which has an all-day unlimited brunch. Rather than give you the name, go search it out for yourself and enjoy the reward of Yelping with intent. I promise, you will not make it beyond three hours. The wait staff is fantastic, and unlike some places, they do not let your glass remain empty for long. Though this particular spot is usually not busy, eventually people will catch on, so be sure to make a reservation.

Then there's the personal drinking time which comes at the end of a long work day or after a shitty date. Most people go to the liquor store closest to their apartment and never stray. Don't fall into this trap, just because it's a close shop does not necessarily mean it's the best option. There are three shops very near my apartment and I like to hop between them.

This is why: The shop nearest me is great for a bottle of vodka or purchases of wine when you grab three or more. The more wine you buy, the larger the discount. There are no deals as far as vodka, but it's always good to know where to grab a quick bottle. The shop furthest from me is open all hours of the day and night. This is where you go when it's way too late for you to still be out, but you have a desire to keep drinking, and wish to ensure your day and head are full of pain when you wake the following morning. The wine shop in between these two is great because it offers a wide selection of red wines, but you earn points for every dollar you spend. [Smiley Emoticon Here!] Yes, you are rewarded for making the decision to drink. You can maximize the reward by making your purchase on a cash back credit card. In this instance you are actually earning money off of alcohol without becoming a bartender. If I was a Buzzed person, I'd be calling this a life hack and sending you fifteen photos of myself with different bottles of wine. Though, that's pretty much what my Facebook timeline looks like. Wine and cat photos.

Keeping in line with personal drinking decisions and behaviors, you'll eventually find a local bar (or six) to call home. There are a few which I love, and it comes down to a few key factors; Internet enabled jukebox. Not only is this device the best thing ever, because you have access to nearly all music, you can also screw with people who pump cash into the machine. See, most electronic jukeboxes have an app for your phone, and when you choose to play a song next via the app it will skip any play-next songs purchased directly on the machine. It's fun to watch people start throwing tantrums when their song never plays.

Bartenders are just as important to the vibe of a bar and your experience. Boiler Room on the Lower East Side is a dank, hole in the wall, always a good time, and the bartenders are always friendly and fast. Along with drink specials, there is no attitude, as some bartenders act as though it is a huge imposition to serve a drink. Not to say people with ridiculous orders are not fully deserving of a scowl, but if you're asking for a beer or a vodka soda it shouldn't be an ordeal. I don't see this happen as often in straight bars, maybe we're just gay bitches and that's the problem. Either way, a smile goes a long way with a cocktail, and also ensures you want to bring friends here once you've decided to call the bar your own.

For those of you who aren't alcoholics, it's wise to always keep some booze in the house. You never know when someone is going to drop by for a visit. There's nothing worse than being the host who has nothing to offer. Keep a bottle of vodka in the freezer, a few beers in the fridge and a couple of bottles of red on the rack. For those of you who are alcoholics: You will need to resist the urge to drink them, and in all honesty, in a pinch you definitely can, but always replenish your stockpile for guests.

The rules of alcohol are not strictly applied to hosts. When you're invited to a party, be it a friend's apartment or someplace new, don't be the douche bag who arrives empty handed. It's probably one of the rudest things people do, arrive with nothing and drink everything. Bring whatever you like to a party, but plan smart. If you aren't sure what kind of party you're attending or what the host may be serving, there is nothing wrong with purchasing what you enjoy and making that your party favor. This means you definitely have something to drink, and if there's something else you like upon arrival, that's a bonus.

You can think of it this way when taking alcohol to a party; Bring two bottles of wine so you can drink one and share the other. Personally, I like to take three because my friends and I all have bottomless livers. It's important to ensure you have access to plenty of alcohol when attending a social gathering in someone's home, because you truly have no idea who else is going to be in attendance and may need to kill your senses.

Other guests can be the best or worst part of going out. For example, I am often invited to certain events only because if the host doesn't invite me, a couple of my friends may not attend. If that's not the case, they're likely to bring me along and there's going to be that awkward moment when I thank the host for my invitation which never arrived. I'm a little bit of a dick, but I mostly just like to poke fun at people when I know it's going to be uncomfortable. How fucked up is that?

When you're interacting with these strangers they're going to ask you where you live, what you do for work, how you know the host, if you're in attendance alone and so on. To survive these useless questions, it's best to keep a drink in your hand at all times. And if you make sure your glass is never too full it becomes easy to excuse yourself for a refill, when in reality all you want is to get away from this person who has invaded your space. Of course, this can give people the perception that you're an alcoholic, now that you're circling the kitchen or bar like a homeless person digging a five-dollar bill out of a storm drain.

You have to make the determination if this bothers you. If it's a problem, you'll want to fill your glass and go sit alone in the corner. How can you be so sensitive and live in this city? Grow some balls and realize it doesn't matter what anyone thinks of you. You're an alcoholic? Good for you! You've just achieved something special, give yourself a pat on the back because people clearly have nothing better to do than spend their time judging you. You're on the right path. If you're really an alcoholic, you can always swing by an AA meeting for coffee and some gossip. Apparently, it's the place to go to get the inside dirt on other people whom you have no connection. And if Romy and Michelle taught us nothing else, it's a great place to meet men.

13. Visitors & Tourists

At some point after the one-year mark of living in the city, people from wherever you come from will begin to visit. You'll get all excited to hang out with friends and family you haven't seen in a hot minute, and you'll spend time scrubbing your apartment and coaching your roommate on how to avoid pissing off whomever is coming by not saying this and that. Take this seriously, as one birthday my mom was visiting and I left her at the table while I went to grab drinks, my roommate said something to her while I was away that set her off. What she said, I have no idea, but my mother came over to me and growled,

"You better shut that little bitch up before I knock her off that bar stool."

When these people come, you may even be so nice as to meet them at the airport, either via train or ZipCar. I suggest the

ZipCar, trust me on this one. It took three years before I got this message and stopped taking the long ass train ride to pick up friends. If you live in the city proper, it's likely to take anywhere from one to three hours to get to JFK. If your guest(s) decided to enter via LaGuardia, the third world of airports according to some [a sentiment most New Yorkers agree with], they should plan to taxi their way to you. There is no excuse for punishing someone with an unnecessary pick up from this horrible airport.

In either case, you end up lugging around oversized bags. This will be the first of the many, many mistakes your guest(s) will make that will piss you off. Even if you are lucky enough to live in an elevator building, you still have to drag their heavy ass suitcases up and down stairs to and from the subway. People will scowl as you knock into them, run over feet and generally piss the world off with your consumption of excessive space. Space is at a premium here and we all feel entitled to all of it, all the time.

Since you didn't grow up in New York, it's safe to assume those who come to visit didn't either. The first thing they'll say when they see your apartment, the one you love because you've painted a little and decorated the place in such a way that you feel perfectly content,

"Wow, it's so small. How much do you pay in rent?"

In this moment you'll want your friend/family member to die. You'll want to take a shank and stab them right in the chest. What do they mean your apartment is small? It's twice the size of the crackerjack box your one friend lives in and it's huge for a studio. These thoughts will race through your mind while a fake smile stretches across your face. Then you generally get an earful on how ridiculous it is you're paying $1,800 or $2,200 a month in rent while 'back home you could own a place for half as much a month.' Settle in because this is only the beginning.

Like everyone else, your guest needs a MetroCard. They'll fork over twenty or so dollars to purchase a pass, which is really a pass to the entire city, such a bargain. As you wait in a hot and sweaty, summer subway station, they'll whine,

"I could never live without a car."

This is the most common word vomit to come from non-New Yorkers. Well, maybe you prefer to not be tied down with a monthly payment for a car and the outrageous cost of insurance. This won't matter, you can dispute the uselessness of owning a vehicle in New York, your guest won't hear a word. They're convinced a car is mandatory to the survival of the human race. Take comfort in knowing they're helping kill the planet with their gas-guzzling SUV and you're a small part of the effort to not be a huge dick. You can also take comfort in knowing you can't get pulled over, get a parking ticket, run out of gas, have a flat tire or have a car stolen. Also, every mile and year makes the car they pay for worth even less. So, your visitor can suck a big car dick, **you win**.

You survive the first day, and this is the point when you realize your visitor is actually a tourist in disguise. The New York economy depends upon the hard earned money of tourists. Unfortunately, no one informed New Yorkers of this as we hate tourists and their annoying habits. They clog sidewalks by stopping in the middle and spreading out to look at subway maps. They are unable to recognize the need for taking off a backpack in subway cars. Tourists knock into you as their eyes are focused up when they need both looking dead ahead to avoid one of us shoving them off a curb into the street. However, when they do look down from the thrill of hovering buildings, they'll tug on your shirt sleeve, even though you're wearing headphones and your face clearly reads, go to hell, to ask for directions. *'Where is Chinatown?'* I use this example as it's the one I've been asked more than any other direction-based question.

Your guest will want to go sightseeing. You have no interest as you have visited everything in the city worth seeing, and the places you've not been, need not be visited because you have zero interest in subjecting yourself to standing in long lines which charge you at the end. They may want to visit the Empire State Building. The view from the top is impressive, you can see every corner of the city. The line on the weekends is so painful you better put some cocktails in your friend's backpack. Don't believe me? There are restrooms at multiple points in this three prong, two elevator line maze. The stewards of your line know you're stuck for long stretches of time and planned appropriately.

Once you reach the top it's a shoving match to get to the edge. Selfie sticks and hands with phones are jolting out in every direction. If and when you reach the edge for your perfect photo opportunity, other tourists will walk in front of the camera, ruining the photo. Also, the wind is almost always blowing up there, so plan to have fucked up hair or wear a hat.

Next you'll find yourself in Central Park. This isn't so bad, or is it? Why is your friend chasing after squirrels in an effort to snap a photo? Central Park is gigantic, and though pedestrian, bike and vehicle traffic are sown together on different levels, they intersect in places, meaning you're darting across lanes of traffic as bicyclists whiz by ringing their little bells at you. Not only are you annoyed by all the people, you're also sweating your ass off because most of the park isn't as shaded as you'd like and the up and down of all the hills will put your shoes to the test.

Forcing your guest out of the park only leads to another destination. They want gifts for friends and family back home. You can find trinket shops almost anywhere, but Chinatown is the place most people want to buy cheap crap. You'll be approached by person after person trying to sell you fake bags. "Gucci? Gucci?" They'll whisper as they attempt to shove paper into your hand. If you don't keep an eye on your guest, it's likely they'll be lead to a van or into a shop where they'll be paying good money for cheap fakes that look like real designer stuff. Not to say you can't get stolen goods in Chinatown, but you need to know where to go, what to say and how to behave. The purchase of stolen goods is truly an art. It's also illegal so don't be stupid, be careful.

As your visitor's presence begins to wear on your nerves, turning a long weekend from a fun idea to a nightmare, you'll begin to pray for their departure. I let most of my guests share my bed, a big deal as I don't even want the people I date sleeping over. This is my bed, stay out of my bubble. You may do the same or stick them on the sofa, either way, in small apartments, when you're no longer living with a roommate it can be stressful to again share space. If you still live with a roommate it's something similar to the end of the world. Now the routine you and the roommate have perfected for the bathroom in the morning, is being disrupted by a random intruder who feels they can come and literally go as they please. They don't follow the schedule! You have a time at which you like to shower at the end of the day. Well, don't get too excited because your guest be enjoying the toilet while you're ready to rinse the day off your face. Literally, what are they doing in there, how long can one sitting take a person?

There will eventually come the glorious moment when the guest(s) must return home. This is when Dial7, the car service, is your best friend. Reserve and pay for a car online and know exactly when your guest is going to be on their way. Yes, you will have a brief moment of the sad as you say goodbye and they get in the car. You may even feel like a bit of a dick for wanting them to go so badly. You really did have a good time and it wasn't all that difficult. Wait, it was a huge pain in the ass. It's all very confusing.

Your New Yorker brain will be delighted by the visit in the sense you reconnected with someone, but you'll be just as glad to see them go. Remember, you moved to the city for a reason, and one of those reasons was to get away from suburban types who didn't understand your way of life.

14. Attitude

What is it they say in that commercial? Maybe she's born with it, maybe she's just an asshole? Something along those lines. Everyone in New York has some sort of attitude, not so much a problem if you are 'in the know.' Everyone here is busy, in a rush, on their way, ten minutes late, not in the mood and focused on themselves. It's a lifestyle choice and if you can last in the city a few years, that lifestyle has a way of consuming you.

See, some people arrive in New York off of a train, plane, boat, bus, whatever, and it's all smiles and giggles. You're prematurely excited for your new television-inspired lifestyle that's going to be so great. You may even be one of those actual happy people who New Yorkers find completely annoying. This is not to say New Yorkers are unhappy, they just won't buy into your around-the-clock cheer. The way you ask strangers on the street, 'how they're doing,' it's annoying and often perceived as fake. This may be in fact, your true personality, it's unfortunate. I'd suggest seeing a professional, anyone who can provide some sort of downer to bring you home to our bleak, shallow reality.

Let's get something straight, I was bitter and cynical long before arriving in New York, as noted previously. In my late teen years, it was common for people to tell me things such as, 'You're too young to be this cynical,' and a personal favorite, 'Don't worry, you'll grow out of it.' Guess what, some people grow into an attitude and even more so when you find the perfect place to feed the flames of bitterness.

Once more, it's worth stating an important fact; New York does not actually have the power to turn you into a bitter asshole. No, this is something which happens over time, it may even sneak up and surprise you. The personality shift may be so subtle that it takes a stranger pointing it out in order for it to become obvious. Once you realize you've been New Yorkitized, you may think, wow, how did that happen? It happens something like this:

You've been out all night and want to go home. You've been waiting on the train platform for half an hour and the L train is finally coming. The doors open and you enter the car, everyone is crammed into one end of the train, which you know is a bad sign. Looking around for a homeless person or a crazed person, you realize you're standing in fresh vomit. The smell didn't reach your nose before the train car's doors closed because you're drunk, and now you're not only part of the mess, you want to kill whomever made the mess. There's nothing you can do but sit down and try to get the vomit off your shoes by dragging them over the hideous plastic floor. It's going to be the longest train ride of your life.

Then there's the time you were at the laundromat, and lucky for you there's an empty dryer, no need to wait in line, you gleefully toss your load inside and shove quarters into the slot to activate the heat beast. Forty-five minutes later, you open the dryer to retrieve the partially dry clothing. That's when you realize there's something black smeared all over your shirts. It's gooey, thick and on everything. Someone before you clearly left something in a pocket that has now ruined two of your favorite shirts, some jeans and numerous other items. You won't throw anything away, but try washing it all two more times before sticking this ruined merchandise in the back of your closet, where it will consume much needed space for the next year. I say a year because it usually takes until the next Spring cleaning binge to come to terms with the loss and get rid of the unwearable items.

These frustrations may push you to move to a new neighborhood, perhaps one with in-building laundry and far away from the L train. You have two options: beg friends to help you move your stuff, or pay three guys to assist with the move. Let's say you pick option two because you have an extra $1,500 you'd like to throw away. Moving companies offer all kinds of deals, usually with some sort of requirement that you pay for three movers and for at least three hours. You'll do all kinds of prep work to have things ready, meaning boxes are packed, stacked and everything is ready to go. Then the movers arrive and move at the speed of death. Not only could they care less about your shit, they are being paid by the hour. That means they are encouraged to move as slow as is humanly possible.

Also, no matter how much packing is done in advance, you're going to get some kind of up-sell. Either a mirror needs to be crated, a television put in a special box or pictures wrapped. Suddenly, there's another three-hundred-dollar fee you haven't accounted for in your moving budget.

Once the movers do finally get the truck loaded, almost every single time, they get lost trying to find your new apartment. Honestly, you could be moving across the street, these guys would circle the block six times, park downstairs and call only to tell you they can't find the building. Most of your belongings are going to be safe and sound, a few scratches and dents, it's more the cost and frustration which will make you realize you've got to start making a lot more money so you can afford a better moving company.

Last, but not least, don't forget to tip. You're expected to tip your movers in cash, and they aren't afraid to ask you for the money. Be prepared for some serious pressure. I try to tip twenty percent for things like this, and still, I was asked to give another ten percent because the stairs in my building are a whore. Your movers, and I notified the company of the stairs, why should I have to increase the tip just because you don't like a workout?

Now you find yourself living in a new apartment and need to get a few things from IKEA. I mean, you just dropped two grand on movers. Not only will you be back on your diet of starvation, but you also can't be shopping in the nicer stores. Brooklyn's IKEA is easiest to get to by way of the subway when living in the city proper, the other locations all require renting a car. I mean, you can ZipCar, but it just gets to be such a hassle with the traffic and all the other cars. You take the G train then a shuttle, arrive at the Brooklyn IKEA, where you wander for a few hours and buy a couple things. You end up buying one or two things too large to carry up the long stairs to the subway station. You decide to take a cab; it's going to cost a fortune but it will save you some frustration. Now you wish you had rented the ZipCar, but it's too late to fix the problem. It's a sick cycle. Cars: Damned if you do, dead if you drive.

Unfortunately, snow began coming down as your cab left the store parking lot. You inch nearer the apartment when the driver hits the brakes just a little too hard, slides off the road and directly into a fire-hydrant. Now, if he hits another car you are forced to stay at the location and wait for a police officer to take a statement. Since you didn't hit a car, you now have the honor of dragging your new merchandise home in the middle of a blizzard. It sucks so hard, but there's nothing you can do but trudge through the snow and get your cheap crap home.

Maybe you don't like shopping for furniture, but you do like going out for drinks with friends. You drink on the West side, and live on the East side, a non-issue during regular train hours. However, it's after midnight and you can take a pricey cab, wait for a train that may never come, or walk your intoxicated ass home. You decide to walk and make the decision to cut through Central Park, but you didn't know the park closed at midnight. This is a real thing, all parks that don't have gates close at midnight.

A cop pulls up to your drunk self and asks what you're doing. Thinking you're funny, you give him some lip. This then turns into standing in front of the patrol car for half an hour while he does whatever with your license. When the cop does finally return you get the prize of a $75 ticket for being in the park after hours, and a friendly warning that next time you'll be spending the night in jail. [That last part may be because I couldn't shut the fuck up when told to do so.]

Seriously, am I the only person who was unaware of the park hours? I mean, I was twenty feet away from 59th Street, is it such a big deal to be in the park at this hour? It's not like I'm in the pushes sucking dick to get some thrills. There actually is a tiny sign, very near the ground with the park hours when you enter from the corner near Columbus Circle. Even sober, I have never noticed the sign, so I feel as though it's an invitation to get in trouble.

These are just a few examples of what's going to get thrown at you. There's also the pushing, shoving, baristas who mess up your coffee, hosts who ignore your reservation, people who yell at you and a million other things. At some point you stop giving a fuck and start pushing back. You yell at people who get in your way, you are not about to let someone take your table at a restaurant and getting spit on is an act of war which will send your bag and fists flying. You're not an asshole, you're a New Yorker.

15. Crime

No matter where you live in this big, crazy world, it's possible to be robbed, crime is a real thing. I was reminded of this today as my straights sent me a text. My straights are a soon-to-be-married couple whom I've known for some time and depend on for drinking games and the comical judgement of others. We're more or less in a three-way sexless marriage. It's practically perfect. [Note: They will actually be man and wife by the time this is published.]

My straights had been vacationing in Puerto Rico to celebrate Rebecca's birthday. She's the lady half of the two, it seems worth sharing as we live in a world where gender is becoming ever more complex, and in case you skipped some of the early chapters it helps to have a name. On their last day in San Juan, it was discovered that someone had broken into their hotel room and stolen all of their cash. Not a pleasant experience, but on the bright side, at least they weren't murdered in their sleep. In that case, who would I drink with? Yes, I'm selfish and they are not allowed to die, solely because I would be left to drink by my lonesome.

Crime exists on all islands, and yes, Manhattan is an island, even though some people seem to think it's not. Having water on all sides, it's an island. Long Island, which has Queens and Brooklyn on one end, also constitutes a true island. Maybe it's all the bridges and tunnels, but I am surprised when people tell me we aren't living on an island. Unless they are somehow referencing the people and meaning to say we aren't truly isolated as individual islands. If that's the case, they're still wrong because the people here are even more disconnected from one another than the chunks of land we call home.

Anyway, you should not feel unsafe in your apartment, unless you're living in an actual crack house, I've yet to know anyone who was robbed or murdered while sleeping. I've only been here a decade, so I suppose this could change, but we'll knock on wood and assume it won't. I do believe people on the street are the ones you should be aware or fearful of, over strangers breaking and entering at random.

A friend, who I won't name as this describes illegal activity and I'm not in the business of getting anyone busted, tried to buy cocaine off one of those street guys. You'll know what I mean the moment you encounter one. They are random guys, usually in well populated areas, who walk close to you and mutter, 'Weed, weed, coke, weed, pills.' If you want it, they've got it tucked in a pocket. In my opinion, you are welcome to snort, swallow or smoke anything you like, but find a real dealer, do not buy from these guys on the street, you're asking for the consequences. If you need a dealer, simply go to any loud night club or dark dance floor and hang near the bathroom. See the guy coming out rubbing his nose, he can point you in the right direction.

So, my friend tries to by coke from this guy. Since he doesn't have enough cash on him, he makes his second huge mistake, having the guy walk with him to the ATM. Don't assume because the ATM vestibule is a brightly lit room with windows that people won't commit a crime. He withdraws the money and here is the point where the guy takes his cash, wallet, phone and roughs him up. I know the details only because immediately after he came to my apartment. Apparently, I'm good in a crisis, who knew. That, or he was so traumatized it made being around a crazier person seem like the right decision.

This is the kind of stuff that happens when you live in a densely populated place. Though it does tend to happen more often to people who make stupid decisions, like taking a stranger with you into an ATM vestibule. I mean, if you hate having money in your bank account, please feel free to send it my way. You need to be aware of your surroundings at all times, not necessarily in a defensive way, but in some way. People who walk with their phones and bump into others, these are prime targets because they're too stupid to pay attention. It is possible to text, walk and know what's going on in front, behind and beside you.

This is where learning to have resting bitch face, if you weren't born with one, comes in handy. People won't ask you for change on the street, a seat on the subway or anything else. It's only when you let the naive, non-city person you are show through, that is the moment you become a mark. This is more about on the street activities than in your apartment. In all honesty, there's not that much you can do to keep people from breaking into a building, aside from trying to pick a good neighborhood where the rents are higher and the buildings are taller. You never hear about rich old ladies on the Upper East Side having strange men crawl through their 30th Floor window unless expressly invited, and then it's usually some sexy roleplaying game.

When you sign a new lease there is a page that asks if there are children under the age of ten living in the apartment. If yes, you can opt to have the window guards installed. If no, you can still opt to have them installed. It annoys the landlord, but it can be the difference between you being robbed or the neighbor next door. Not that you want your neighbor to be robbed, but face reality, if it must happen to one of you, you sure as hell don't want it to be you. Bars on the window are the quickest and most effective way to keep people out. It's like prison, except you get to go out for coffee in the morning and no one is trying to rape you in the shower.

What you can't keep out are the people you know. I think everyone is inclined to take something which isn't theirs as some point in life. Maybe you're like my niece and lifting earrings from the mall. A petty crime, but stupid when you consider the number of cameras watching at any given moment in a public setting. What came as a shock to me as far as theft, was when a cock ring went missing from my apartment. A cock ring, for those who don't know, is something you slide over your penis, fitting it around the base of the penis and testicles. The goal is to have a longer, stronger erection, and sometimes it's just for fun.

This particular cock ring was neat because it was made of a stretchy silicon and had a vibrating bullet on one end, which rested under the testicles to provide an extra buzzy thrill. I decided to use the clinical words over cock and sack here because I'm pretty sure one or two people who know me are going to read this and be grossed out by the thought. Going to get the cock ring one day, I noticed it was missing from my goody drawer. I poked around, eventually figuring I had misplaced the damn thing. It wasn't for several weeks that it came to mind. Visiting a friend's apartment, wouldn't you know I saw the exact same cock ring sitting on his nightstand. Now, I didn't take it back, there is a slim chance we both purchased the same one, as mass production means we can all have the same things in life. But it seems a little farfetched that we'd end up with the same one because it was ordered special off of a particular website.

Sex toys are not all you have to worry about having lifted from your apartment. I'm not religious in any capacity, which you probably figured out from the last paragraph if not from the entire book, but I do wear a cross. I have two favorites and interchange them with frequency. Both crosses went missing right around the time I had a falling out with a friend. There was no evidence he took them, but seeing as I'm pretty sure he stole the cock ring, a cross didn't seem that far behind.

I actually did find one of the crosses a year later in the back of a drawer, it had slid out from where I usually stored them. Hoping this was the fate for both I tore apart the dresser drawers looking for the second cross. The favorite cross has been missing for just over three years, and I can say with certainty it is not in my apartment, as I have now moved twice during the time it's been gone and have packed and unpacked all my belongings. I firmly believe it is tucked in my friend's apartment somewhere. He knows how much it pisses me off not having it, and considering we are only back to being semi-friends, it could be getting him off to know he's got two things I enjoy.

The warning here is really just to watch your back. The people you know can screw you, and the people you don't know can really screw you. If you don't want to show up at a friend's place in the middle of the night crying about your stolen wallet and phone, don't be an idiot, keep your eyes open and know who's around you at all times.

16. Fit Shit

People outside of major metropolitan areas may not be able to say this, "All of my friends have a gym membership." It's true, all of my friends are a member of one gym or another. One teaches weekly spin classes, a feat which blows my mind when we are both mid-hangover from going out the night before until way beyond our bed times. Yes, the gym is something you need to get comfortable with in a big city.

This is one expense that can become a sort of addiction. In New York City there are hundreds, and possibly thousands, of people who you will pass each day and compare yourself to. These random people may be skinnier, taller, prettier, have better skin, hair, nails, clothing, whatever; there is a multitude of things that will lower your self-esteem as you compare yourself to people with whom you will likely never even converse. Though knowing this will not prevent it from happening. Again, as so many times before in this little train wreck of a book, a trained psychologist would likely point out this behavior as being unhealthy.

Obviously. Half the behaviors that make it possible to not only survive, but to thrive, in the city are emotionally and mentally unhealthy. That never stops any of us...but it does keep the pharmaceutical industry in a profitable position.

Picking a gym can be nearly as painful as getting yourself to use the gym for which you are paying to be a member. There are a range of prices and services, though I will refrain from using the specific gym names, as they seem more likely to sue with their big law firms and teams of lawyers standing on the sidelines. Let's begin at the top and work our way down the price chain.

There is only one gym chain in the city which will charge you $250 or more for your signup fee, and this is generally a discounted price. You'll also be paying just as much for your monthly membership. Yes, this gym offers clean locker rooms and fancy shampoo, but is it really worth the cost? Seriously, if you want me to pay what would realistically be equal to my monthly coffee budget to lift weights and run on a treadmill, you better be injecting me with some steroids or lifting the damn weights on my behalf.

This gym is like a spa hybrid which will feed on your bank account. You really can live without the super strong smelling shampoo and conditioner they offer up, honestly, it's not doing you that much good. Though their marketing is attractive, seeing as it's hot naked people almost all the time. The reality is most of us will never look like the super-hot math teacher in the ads. I know, it sucks, but that's what happens when you have a life and enjoy things like alcohol.

Another, smaller chain, offers similar services, with a slightly less painful fee, but it feels like you're working out in an Abercrombie store. Having tried this gym on one occasion by way of a friend's invitation, it smelled strongly of cologne and all of the impressively ripped people inhabiting the space rarely lifted a weight. They did however spend an insane amount of time lifting their shirts in front of mirrors to snap photos, which probably ended up on social sites for the consumption of others. Though I don't know this to be true, but can believe it so, the locker rooms and sauna for this particular brand are a breeding ground for blowjobs. Next time you're taking a shower be sure to keep the flip flops on to avoid picking up any unwanted joy juice.

This is the gym I would join if I really wanted to feel bad about myself. The members are insanely attractive and built, but I assume they are probably models and actors. If I had no full-time job, I'd probably be at the gym for six hours a day as well. I'd work on my form, get super ripped and walk around half naked while pretending to be deep. Just kidding, if I didn't have a full-time job I'd move into the bar on the corner and only leave once they stopped extending me credit.

Moving down on the monthly fee scale we come to the gym which shares its name with an abdominal exercise. This was my gym for about two years before I left for another. On the whole this gym is an okay price, if you are only using a single location, and again offers many amenities, along with blowjobs in the locker rooms. This is the place you want to be if group fitness is your shtick. There are tons of classes, but make sure you sign up in advance or your ass will be watching from the hallway.

What is incredibly annoying about this gym is the training staff. If you ever show up outside of peak hours to workout you are likely to be engaged. It seems innocent when a trainer offers some advice on your form, or even when they ask if they can test a routine on you. **Just say no.** Like rape or most drugs, you don't want what they have to offer. They are preparing to try and sell you on a package, which is by no means cheap. Unless you are planning to drop a grand and be guilt ridden by this stranger, just say no and walk away from them with haste.

Last but not least, we have my first gym in the city. With the most locations of any gym in the area, you get a little bit of everything: Pools, 24-hour locations and like Starbucks, a location accessible on nearly every corner. Because this gym costs the least of all the competitors it has a more ghetto perception. Having visited many locations, I don't totally disagree, but it does depend upon which location you call home, as to what will be your experience.

This particular chain of gyms isn't always the cleanest as the staff doesn't seem too thrilled by their work. The trainers can be certified after a five-day course, I know this because I spent the $200 and took the course. When I was twenty-two I thought I wanted to be a personal trainer. After completing the course and written exam, I was placed in a real live gym with no experience and expected to sign-up clients and begin working them out. At the time I was about one-hundred and thirty pounds of scrawny, in no reality should I have been allowed on the floor as a trainer. It wasn't my small stature that made me quit, it was realizing I'd have to work with people. I hate people, my years of retail helped me learn this fun fact, though I failed to make the connection when I began to pursue personal training.

It may seem like it would be easier to skip the gym altogether. I mean, wouldn't it be better to spend your free time exploring the city and hanging out with friends over a couple of beers? Yes, yes it would, but if you ever want to get laid, you best get yourself to the gym on the regular. As mentioned previously, the other people in our fair city are here for the purpose of making you feel inferior, they aren't here to build you up. Yes, your friends may provide this exciting service of self-esteem building to you, but no stranger is going to be so kind.

Now you think I'm a fat shaming dick. I suppose you can make this assumption about me and that's okay if it's your opinion. I'm just trying to save you the frustration of realizing you have to join a gym, before you gain the twenty pounds that come with all the amazing food lurking around every corner. No matter where you decide to live in the five boroughs, or whom you choose to hang out with, you are going to end up eating and drinking [a lot]. This is why it's best to get into the habit of working out right from the beginning of your life in the city.

If you are on a tight budget, which all of us are, there are ways to workout without breaking the bank up front and splurging on a year-long gym membership. *Parks* - they are literally everywhere! You know what is inside of all parks?

Running paths to help you get in tune with nature and burn off all those drinks from last night. And if you are so inclined to be around other people, there are tons of free outdoor yoga and fitness classes in which to participate. All you need to do is open up the web browser on your phone and do a quick search.

I will give one final warning, no matter how fit you are, there is always going to be someone with a better body. Don't focus on comparing yourself to others, especially the models running around the city, it will literally drive you insane. Realize that it only matters that you like your body. Confidence is pretty sexy and that's what will draw people to you, it's also what's going to catapult you into being a true New York asshole, so don't get too cocky. I also apologize for ending this chapter on an upbeat note. I promise, it will not happen again.

17. Clickers

In New York City, we are all individuals. Individuals in the sense that we are all responsible for our own life, bills, jobs, etc. I am of course excluding any siamese twins living in the city, if there are any, as they would technically be a twosome. Which makes me wonder, would the government tax them twice if they worked a single job? Would they need to file taxes as two different people, even though they share a majority of a single body? I'm also excluding anyone who is taking advantage of city programs to avoid work, fund their inability to use contraceptives and pretty much piss everyone off with their entitlement. Those aren't individuals, those are assholes.

You may think this is picking on the unfortunate people of our city. No, it's not. One of my friends is one of these people and it makes me nuts. He's a working photographer, but will only accept cash payments because he has learned how to work the system. He gets a check from the government every week to help cover his food and rent. He isn't living in a palace, but he sure has a lot less stress than the people I know who go to work every day and bust their asses. People like him are the ones I'm excluding, a.k.a, the assholes.

Most people think of being an individual as having a unique something about something. Perhaps it's your edgy style, that amazing haircut and color, the artsy job which pays little but is truly fulfilling, etc. In reality, everything and everyone has been done before, there is no true individuality any longer, it's just how you chose to live your life. No matter how "different" or "unique" a person claims to be, there will always be a way to lump you into a pre-existing group. Some view this as a terrible thing, if you fit into a box you're a conformist and everything is terrible. In fact, fitting into a box just makes it easier to find people with similar interests and make friends.

Here's an example: If you like Starbucks instead of local coffee, you are a sellout to major corporations and a pawn. A pawn for what exactly has never been clear. Mainly because anyone I've ever heard make this claim is a hipster douche living off of their parents' money. Why do I like Starbucks? Well, how great is it to know I can walk into a location in any state, territory or country, place my order and receive the exact same drink. This is not to say one can't have a cup of local coffee now and again, but for me it's a pain in the ass to deal with whatever a coffee shop is doing to be unique. Like the time when I asked for a medium vanilla latte and the barista of this particular local shop asked me if I wanted a half or full shot of vanilla. Thinking a shot would be equal to a single pump of vanilla, I asked for a full shot. The barista proceeded to put twelve pumps, you read correctly, of vanilla into my drink. It was horrifically terrible in taste and consistency.

I've since given up vanilla and prefer plain lattes these days, but it's still better to get them from Starbucks. I also started buying stock in the company because of how much coffee I consume. It's a tiny way of giving back to myself, though this is completely irrelevant to the point. This problem will present itself more so when you're on a date and suggest the chain coffee shop for the meeting place. If you are going out with a hipster, you are fucked. Oh lord, you are so fucked. Fucked with a capital see you next Tuesday. You'll either get a cancellation, or you're going to have to hear all about how big companies are destroying the world.

I'm in the middle on how I feel about big corporations, I can see their value and they shouldn't be punished for being successful. Yet, I can also see the value of keeping big box stores out of places like New York, where there are tons of small businesses that would not be able to compete. I mean, I'm not a complete monster. Coffee is just one example where you are going to be made painfully aware of people's preferences and obsessions. But this hipster date person is going to make your head hurt with all their reasons for why corporations are the devil. In reality, they probably go home and use hairspray while masturbating to live streaming porn. That's twice as evil as drinking a cup of yummy Starbucks coffee.

Bars can be as bad as coffee shops. You have the craft beer drinkers, the winos, the dive bar lovers, the foodie drinkers and so many more. These are the groups which look down on you for being in any of the other groups and will give you a shit ton of useless knowledge about their preferred drink/food in an effort to let you know they're better than you. Yes, they are better than you. Why? Because they go home and write Yelp reviews about what poor service they received in a busy restaurant during the busiest time of day, and how the wine tasted bad even though they've never had a red wine touch their lips before that moment.

None of these clicky bastards compare to the fashionistas. These people are the worst of the worst. They're always dressed nicely, sometimes a little over the top, they live in a bubble of self-made credit card debt or on the dime of their daddy. If you want to meet a truly snobby, asshole of a person, just walk down 5th Avenue. These are the people who come to New York, thinking they will be living in an episode of Sex and the City. In an effort to replicate the lifestyle of our favorite television characters they spend, belittle and bark at anyone they cross. There may have once been decent people under the layers of cloth, and a few do manage to remain as tolerable human beings, but for the most part these purse-lipped people are difficult to tolerate. Expect to feel bad for wearing last year's jeans when you're out with this type of person, you'll likely think you're in the Movie, Mean Girls.

I will say you must not wear sweat pants out in public. This is a personal issue; I have on more than one occasion told someone they couldn't go somewhere with us for wearing sweat pants. Sweat pants are for the gym and your bedroom. They do not belong on a city sidewalk where everyone can see. This is not me being a snob, [it's me being a bitch] it's just me sharing a little bit of information so you can avoid looking like a fool. It will also save you from having someone shout, *"You can't sit with us!"*

If you are gay, like myself, you are going to get a giant dose of the gays. There is every type of gay in the city, honestly, I think the diversity in gay culture trumps straight culture, no offense. Gays are colorful, but there are the gays like me who are loud and toned down, meaning I run my mouth but pretty much have an all-black wardrobe. Then there are the gays who feel they need to ensure everyone knows they are gay. This comes in many forms and I'm going to catch a lot of shit for putting this group in a box, but here goes: There are the over-the-top gays who are wearing makeup, glitter, ultra-colorful clothing, sometimes clothing made for the opposite gender, all while running around making sure everyone notices them and then being mad when people talk shit.

Gays can be intense and intimidating, especially when you are one. I've been to more than one cocktail party where I'm the loud, drunk gay, it's pretty much my thing. But I'm also known for ghosting, I go home without people noticing when I realize I'm trashed. There are the other gays who like to be loud, proud and terrifying. These gays are a singular parade walking down the street to the beat of their own drum on the daily. These are also the gays which I try to avoid as they do not click with me. In fact, when we come together, it's like a nuclear bomb has gone off and someone is going to be verbally assaulted. Throw some vodka on us and let the fire rage.

The city is full of clicks, good or bad, and you fall into many of them, it's not an option, it's a reality. I say, find the ones that fit you best and embrace that which is you. Yes, it means your acceptance by one group/click excludes you from being a part of another group/click, but sometimes that's for the best. It's like high school, no one person belongs to every group, except for the head cheerleader, that bitch belongs in every group in high school. The good news there is she never makes it out of Kansas, and is saddled with four kids and two divorces by the time she turns thirty. This also means you can take some satisfaction in knowing the bitch who made you feel like shit back in the day is jealous of your awesome life. [You know she's going to be stalking you online.] Pretty sure that's not what you're supposed to do, as we are all supposed to love each other in our modern age, but be realistic, most of us can't stand one another. Find your click and stay there.

18. Must See

It's fairly common for people to ask you, when they come to visit or while in conversation, what are your favorite places to visit. I can't say exactly when a majority of tourist attractions lose their appeal for the newcomer, but usually it happens pretty quick. However, there are a few places every single person in this city should be enjoying with frequency, and many others which I've not made it to yet.

Coney Island: Luna Park has an appeal of its own, classic amusement park charm, desperate to reclaim a former glory that was lost along with the original park grounds years ago when fire claimed the rides and shops. One of the original rollercoasters, the Cyclone, still stands today as a testament to the former glory of the park and continues to be a personal favorite. On last check it cost nine bucks for a ride which only lasts a couple of minutes. You'll leave the ride with a back aching from being jerked around, but it's one of the best rides available. Keep in mind, we're not talking six flags, you need to think slightly less commercial to appreciate the park.

The spook house, though truly for children is another personal favorite, which you should ride after two or three drinks on the boardwalk. Not so much scary, but comical, you're guaranteed to fall into a fit of laughter, post drinks. Wander the park and find your favorite rides, but be sure to save time for the boardwalk. Before taking a long stroll, grab margaritas and then make your way to Nathan's. The reason I suggest having one drink before downing a giant beer and hotdog is because the lines are insane. You will be in line no less than half an hour - on a slow day. During the Mermaid Parade, which is also a must, you can be in line for up to an hour. It's worth the wait and the calories.

If the crowds aren't for you, Battery Park may be more your speed. Located just beyond the World Trade Center complex it is a stark contrast to the city. Once you cross the complex and find yourself beside the Hudson River, you no longer hear the noise of traffic and tourists. Suddenly there are more locals, people walking calmly, enjoying a book on a bench and the salty smell of sea air. In the distance you can see the Statue of Liberty, Governor's Island and of course Jersey, though I doubt that's the view you'll find interesting. If you must look at Jersey, note the Colgate Clock. Yes, there is a giant clock which reminds us of a different time, when there was a factory on the grounds, though I should probably confirm my historical facts on that one.

If you are a history nerd, like myself, you'll love the Financial District. I highly recommend the Boroughs of the Dead walking tour of Lower Manhattan. Not only will you get a dose of the haunted history which shaped the tip of our city, but you'll see where the one and only witch trial took place in New York. You'll walk past a pub where patriots of the time gathered secretly to relay messages to George Washington, who was, at the time, exiled from the city (New Amsterdam). The pub has its own museum with some pretty interesting history, and many rumors of ghosts in the basement and upper floors. Sadly, I've yet to see one, no matter how often I go get drunk in their bar. I have however seen spots, though this cannot be attributed to the super natural.

As far as parks and New York City go, everyone instantly thinks of Central Park, and why not? It's enormous and smack in the middle of this growing metropolis. I suggest making your way to the far North portion of the park. You'll know you're where I'm referring when the lawns are no longer heavily manicured. Yes, we do pay less attention to this portion of the park because it reaches beyond the Upper East and West Sides proper where fewer white people live. That's my opinion, there could be another reason, but I'm pretty sure as more white people move to that end of the park, which falls well above 90th Street, you'll see more money and maintenance pumped into the area.

This area of the park is incredible, built to mimic the Adirondack Mountains, you come to many points where you can no longer see building which are only a few hundred feet beyond the trees. You can hear the trickling water of streams that have been hidden beneath your feet and nature actually appears to exist within this space. Though the concrete jungle thrives all around, there are small animals and tons of birds. If you are into bird watching the park's conservancy, located on the Northeast corner, hosts many free bird watching tours as well as information tours. They last about ninety minutes, but they're free, so don't be a lazy asshole, go learn something.

Governor's Island is another place to visit, but summer is the only time it's worth the trip downtown. There are free summer concert and getting there by way of a ferry is free of charge. Considering the price of a single subway ride, it's worth taking a free ride anywhere you can. You'll notice the terminal is a little more rustic than the fancy, far newer, Staten Island Ferry Terminal, sitting next door. Enjoy the throwback charm of yesteryear and cross the small expanse of water. Aside from concerts there's a former military installation you can wander around and explore. It makes for an interesting day.

The one thing I force everyone to do when they come to visit me, and this is by far the most important thing you can do, walk the Brooklyn Bridge. This may sound a bit odd, but I do suggest making this important walk on a chilly day when there is a threat of rain. I know, I know, you're going to get wet and fuck up your hair. Don't worry, it doesn't look that great even on your best days. Toss on a hat, grab an umbrella, but for the love of god do not put on one of those trash bag ponchos tourists wear. Not only do we all laugh at you, to your face, we also have a strong desire to push you into oncoming traffic.

You must walk the Bridge from Brooklyn to Manhattan, for a reason my mother pointed out in no uncertain terms; It's the best fucking view. You can take the A or C train to High Street, but exit towards the front of the train. There's an awesome little Russian diner, where you can grab breakfast, as you definitely want to be doing this at the beginning of your day. Once fed and properly caffeinated you begin the walk up the long path leading to the base of the bridge. Do pay close attention as there is a clear walking lane and the bicyclists are huge cock faces.

Keep your eyes moving, you'll see creepy landmarks like the Watch Tower building where the Jehovah's Witnesses convert others and pump out their propaganda pamphlets. They are leaving the area if I heard correctly, so by the time you read this the building may be luxury condos. As if Dumbo, that's the neighborhood, needs more overpriced shit none of us can afford.

More familiar buildings like One World Trade, Empire State Building, Chrysler Building and the new pencil tower of Midtown will come into view. Governor's Island to your left and the giant white ventilation building for the Brooklyn-Battery Tunnel, which you may have seen on the news when it flooded during Hurricane Sandy. To your right the Manhattan and Williamsburg Bridges, as different in appearance as the neighborhoods which they connect to one another.

Upon reaching the stone towers of the BK bridge, you will find placards with a detailed history of how the bridge was constructed. Worth taking the ten minutes to read them all. Lots of death and drama brought the ambitious project to life. A fun fact not shared here, but fairly well known, the base of the bridge on the Brooklyn side was once a rather large wine cellar. And I've read, though cannot confirm, the base on the Manhattan side is still filled with food. Reserves from the Cold War days, but again, this is rumor and I've not been able to confirm it to be true, but love the idea.

In the Fall, get on the wine tour circuit. The vineyards of Long Island offer all kinds of packages, including car service, to take you and your alcoholic friends around to a number of vineyards. It's not the finest wine you'll ever consume, but it's pretty good as far as North American wines go. Personally, if its red, I'll take a big glass. Though you may want to come prepared to your wine tour car or van with a small speaker for phones. Almost every time I've been on this tour there has been an issue with the stereo, and it can be incredibly irritating. Remember: The driver doesn't give a shit if the stereo works or not, you're on your own.

It's a big city, explore and find the places to start creating your own list. Don't fall into the habit of only going to the same parks, same museums and same restaurants. If you're going to do that, do us all a favor and go live on Staten Island. Time will stand still with you over there.

19. A Jersey Thing

New Jersey. The name may conjure thoughts of housewives and drama or over-tanned twenty-somethings, binge drinking, humping and fighting. Most of the time everything coming out of Jersey is drama, and loud, oh so loud. Not to say New Yorkers aren't loud, but Jersey folk have a special brand of noise coming from them that is unique.

Having lived in Jersey City for a short time I can say that was enough, you remember from earlier chapters, nothing fancy. You have to ride the PATH Train into the city, which is not part of the New York City Subway and has different fares, and unless things have changed, their own card for entry. [Recently, I discovered you can use a NYC MetroCard on the Path. A huge improvement.] Honestly, I can't even recall if the PATH runs all night, I swear I was unable to be out past midnight when living out there, but maybe that's changed as well. Keeping up on Jersey and their transit is not something I put on my to-do list.

Now, there are some obstacles you will face with friends. This may come as a surprise, it did to me, but it's not possible to ensure everyone stays exactly where they are. It's crazy, everyone wants to evolve and grow as human beings, complete bullshit. It starts off simply when one or two friends move to Astoria.

Let's talk about Astoria for a moment. I swear to god, if one more person I know moves there I'm going to scream. Astoria is a neighborhood within Queens, fairly accessible via the N, R, Q trains, unless you want to go there in the evening or on a weekend, plan to wait. There has been a rush of people fleeing to the area because of the cost effective rent, larger apartments and growing number of restaurants. Okay, I moved into the city proper to escape the transit stress of living in the outskirts, which is worth the increase in rent and diminished space. Though you can't tell this to an Astoria resident, they are obsessed with the neighborhood. I've seen normal Queens hating people move and convert. It's like someone finds Jesus and then they suddenly forget they were previously a cum guzzling, gutter slut.

I'm going to laugh if the 2nd Avenue subway ever opens because the Q train, currently the express line to Astoria, will be rerouted to 96th Street. Meaning, unless one of our defunct train lines is resurrected, service to the area will be diminished. Made more painful because so many people are flocking to the area. Laugh at me now for dealing with a crowded 6 train, your day will come!

When someone who lives in the city moves to an outer borough it can be a bit of a shock. You'll ask yourself, as well as the person making the move, why? They'll have their reasons, all are probably valid, or at the very least they are probably logical. This does not mean you have to like their reasons, but you will have to accept them. The morning my Straights confessed to me they would be moving to Jersey I was stunned. These two are as city as I.

What would push them to make the transition, to cross water, to ruin our lives? Saving $900 a month in rent is the biggest factor. That's a pretty decent amount of money when you consider their new apartment is bigger, has outdoor space and other amenities they currently go without. Though, if I could afford $3,500 a month in rent, I would take their Chelsea apartment in a second. It's in a good location, has a ton of space, has a working elevator and is across the street from a bar which tolerates our extreme alcohol abuse. Assuming we don't play Journey on the Jukebox.

There's no changing the mind of another city dweller once it's been made. You can beg and plead, but unless you are willing to get out the duct tape and perform a late night kidnapping, you're stuck. It's best to make peace with the situation and remind your friends when you do go to visit and they tell you to stop complaining about the amount of time needed to get to wherever, that your bitching is their fault. You had to ride two trains, taking more than an hour out of your day, all in the name of drinking. It's worth it, but you're going to bitch because it's your right as the person who stayed where they belong.

Okay, the commute isn't really that bad, I just hate change.

20. Welcome

You've made it to the end, good for you, you're not illiterate and have the attention span of a seven-year-old. C'mon, you didn't think I was going to let you enjoy the fact that you've reached the end, did you? Really though, congrats on suffering though all the bullshit I've tossed your way. That's exactly what living in New York City is about, taking all this awful shit that happens day in and day out.

Perhaps it would have been best to explain more about myself in the first chapter, but doing so at the end means you've already judged me and formed your own opinions, as you should. Isn't that what every media outlet and personality is telling you; Think for yourself, be your own person, just make sure it's the person we want you to be and the thoughts we've pumped into your head. Now I can say I have contributed to the pollution of your mind. You are truly welcome.

Anyway, coming to New York is not an easy decision, when you think about it in a completely practical manner. I never thought of it in a practical manner, it was a no brainer. You pack your shit and walk away from the life you know for the life you want. That's the same reason you picked up this book and read some or all of it, because you want to absorb everything that is New York. More or less, I could stamp New York on a big piece of dog pooh, smear it on a canvas and call it city art only to know there's some other crazy, New York loving weirdo like myself who will purchase this sewage art.

Once you've made your decision, made your move, you may, like me, think: What the fuck was I thinking? I'm poor, all alone, hungry, cranky and lost half the time. Then the pieces start to click. Which is another reason why I wrote this little book of essays. I wish someone had given me a heads up to some of the bullshit that would be coming my way when I was a new arrival. I know, it's not about having someone hold your hand, but it would have been nice to know how often and hard the city would be kicking me in the balls. It still happens on the regular, that never changes.

Then there is a moment in your New York life where things suddenly click. It might be the first time you're able to give flawless directions, which include a bus and two train transfers. Maybe it's having a deli which knows your order by heart and has it ready to go the moment you walk through the door. Or, Starbucks, maybe the barista you flirt with, but have no interest in, has your order ready to go the moment you walk in, even if you didn't use mobile order. That's love right there. It could be when you're standing in your goal apartment, looking out the window as a neighbor throws a full bottle of wine at his girlfriend on the street below. As he said, "She's being a stupid fucking bitch and should just go," his words. If you didn't realize, that last one was my moment.

Things will click. You'll have been in the city a few years, you'll have established friendships and some work connections, earned yourself a position with a steady income allowing you to move out of the slum building and into something decent or at the very least safe. Suddenly all the stress, tears, fighting and drama are worth it because you feel at home. Yes, we are being sappy for this one second in time.

What you do have to watch out for now is your feeling of complacency. This recently claimed two of my friends as they announced plans to leave the city. Fortunately for me, they've only moved across the Hudson to Jersey City. Not my ideal situation for us, but at least they aren't in another state, or worse, another country. We can still brunch and play, and yes, on occasion I may break my rules and even cross water for them. Actually, I may have to take my Starbucks barista comment back, that last statement is true love, the other is just espresso love.

I too caught a bit of the complacency bug recently. New York stopped challenging me and it felt like I'd conquered the island, if it can be conquered. Maybe it felt more like it just stopped raping my soul with every turn of a corner. An opportunity with work arose, the option to move to Puerto Rico for six months. Now, I didn't give up my apartment, like any wise person I sublet the place to save on rent and ensure I have a place when it's time to come home. I moved down to San Juan and enjoyed the sun. While my friends suffered through a horrible winter, I had the beach two blocks away and plenty of cocktails to occupy the time. However, San Juan is not New York.

Obviously these two places are drastically different, but within the first month of being gone I realized how much I depend upon the city. My entire lifestyle is sown into what the city has provided. No more can I get delivery on demand, or any food delivery for that matter. Service is slow in the sense that you can easily wait an hour before a waiter will bring you a menu. Something about the relaxed lifestyle, there is no rush here. Ever. Everything is done in person, most businesses do not have a website, and when they do it has the functionality of 1996. Makes me think back on the days when we had to pop an AOL disk into the computer for free hours of dial up internet access. If you're under twenty-five you probably have no idea what I mean. Google: **AOL CD 300 FREE HOURS.**

All the luxuries the city offers up, around the clock, gone in the blink of an eye. I did a decent job of making it through, but there is one thing that can't be replicated, the people. The friends you make in New York, as noted previously, are some of the best you'll find. More evident, as said friends made an effort to come visit me in my beach paradise. New Yorkers are a different breed and worth the time and maintenance. Truly, if you find the right friends, maintenance is like a car requiring an oil change. People being the cars and wine being the oil.

And to keep this short and sweet, my rambling making me all kinds of nostalgic, I hope that if you are new to the city, or going on your something number of years, don't forget why you love this crazy place. It won't always love you back, and like any relationship, you're going to end up doing most of the work. In the end you're going to be glad you came. Welcome to New York.

But still, fuck you Taylor Swift. I love you.

Other Works

The Other Realm

The Other Realm: Blood Vengeance

The Anomaly

Rent (minus) Control

Rent (minus) Control: Turning Thirty

Rent (minus) Control: Bulletproof

Dust in the Wind

For more information, visit: www.rbwinters.com

Synopsis

Moving to New York City is the worst decision you'll ever make. Unless you're like a certain, *Welcome to New York*, singer who arrived with millions of dollars and legions of screaming fans. You're going to live in the equivalent of a shack **[shit hole]**, suffer through moronic roommates **[personal death]**, be broke off your ass **[literally]**, and all while trying to prove to the world **[yourself]** you can make it in the big city. You can call it a day and crawl back to wherever you hail from or you can put on your big girl panties and survive. For those of us who survive **[this book is a survival guide]**, we thrive and that's why no matter how badly the city sucks **[the life out of you]** it's the only place worth calling home.